A NOVELLA

WILLA DREW

Published by: Moving Words Publishing

www.movingwordspublishing.com

Cover: Books and Moods

(@booksnmoods on Instagram)

Artwork: María Peña

(@me.me.pe on Instagram)

Printed in the United States of America

STAR STRUCK

ISBN: 978-1-957897-00-4

First Edition: April 2022

STAR STRUCK

A ROMANCE

WILLA DREW

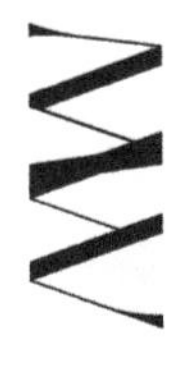

MOVING WORDS PUBLISHING

Join the mailing list for updates and follow Willa Drew on
www.willadrew.com

If you like this book, please consider giving it a review, so others can enjoy it as well.

CONTENTS

For Estelle,

You inspired us to give Siobhan her own story.

★ ★ ★

Tonight on *Extra*.

Maria Fernandez: Maria Fernandez here covering the prestigious Starlight Foundation Gala. On the red carpet with me is Asher Menken, star of romantic comedies like *Legally Hot* and the now-classic heartwarming historical tale *Tomorrow's Love*. Such a pleasure. It's been a couple of years since anyone on this side of the pond interviewed you. Where have you been?

Asher Menken: Thank you for the glowing introduction. Glad to be back in LA. I've enjoyed what the stages of Dublin and London have to offer, but I sure missed the California sunshine.

Maria Fernandez: We're glad to have you back. Hopefully, for good?

Asher Menken: For a while. My project—a collaboration with the winners of this year's Starlight competition—is the first movie my production company will take on. And I have my own reasons to stick around for the next nine months.

One

Siobhan

A cardboard tube with a shred of toilet paper mocks me. Of course, I end up in the bathroom stall that's missing the key element. My parents ran out of Irish luck when they had me: I'm the only member of the Casey clan born on US soil.

"Can't open the flippin' holder." My best friend isn't her usual happy-go-lucky self. She's nervous for a reason. Months of hard work, and the possibility of writing for a big Hollywood movie comes down to tonight.

"Don't break your new nails. Just shove a bunch under the divider."

The coveted wad of white toilet paper and Sarah's undamaged red nails appear beside the spike of my stiletto.

"Got it." My voice sounds strangled, because I'm holding the bottom of my floor-length sequined dress between my chin and my chest.

"Good. Now hurry. We don't want to miss the opening number," says Sarah. "I hope we'll be celebrating more than just your birthday tonight."

The best birthday present would be hearing, "And the Starlight award goes to Sarah Connor." Ever since I met her two years ago when she moved to LA, Sarah's been the one with a plan: become a screenwriter. May have hit a few bumps (okay, craters) on the road, but my girl is making her dreams come true.

The shapewear I have on at the insistence of Mrs. Marino, my boss who lent me this elaborate golden gown worth a year of my salary, doesn't want to go back up. How do people spend all night in these things?

"We were so sorry to hear about you and Leyla," the interviewer says on the TV in the lounge part of the restroom.

My ears perk up. I'm not sorry at all. I've been obsessing over my favorite romantic star's newfound freedom for weeks now.

"Well," Asher Menken's deep baritone loses its smoothness, "all I can say is—"

"Ladies and Gentlemen"—the TV switches from the pre-recorded interview to the real-time coverage of the awards ceremony—"welcome to the Fifth Annual Starlight Foundation Gala."

For feck's sake. The world is dying to know Asher's take on his ex. Okay, I'm dying to know. Even if I get a chance to see him, it's not like I could ask him myself.

"How much longer?" Sarah can't hide her impatience. "I don't want to miss anything."

"Just go." I wave my free hand at the closed door as if Sarah can see me. "I'll be in as soon as I can wrangle this tiny torture device back onto my crotch."

"You sure?"

"Aye, go already. Nick's waiting." Probably cursing me. Boyo is also nervous tonight, and we don't get along at the best of times. "Enjoy yourself. You've worked so hard for tonight."

A few clicks of her high heels plus the sound of the door closing, and I'm left alone with my tight beige nemesis.

I tuck the bottom of the dress into my décolleté. This is bollocks. I peel the undergarment off my thighs and balance on one, then the other silver strappy sandal as I struggle to free myself. Dress righted, I take my first deep breath of the night, ball up the offending material, toss it into the bin, give it the finger, and exit the stall.

A quick check of my stomach in the mirror shows it's as flat as it was with the awful contraption. I wash my hands and ensure my hair survived the battle of the bulge. The aquamarine dye I've been using this summer is starting to bore me. Might be time for a change.

The blue corner of the tattoo on the inside of my wrist is showing. I tug the long sleeves of the dress down, causing the neckline to plunge even more. Gotta make sure I cover up my body art tonight. While highly unlikely, Mum and Da might see pictures. They don't exactly know about this version of my artwork. My tastes run more towards black ink than gold sequins, but I do rock this dress. I blow myself a kiss in the mirror. Time to get this show on the road.

I reach for the door handle when the painted wood panel flies open and smashes into my shoulder. For a moment I teeter on my heels, sure I can save myself, but this battle I don't win. I land hard on the solid tiles of the bathroom floor.

"Bloody hell," I yelp.

The door slams shut, then opens again, and a tuxedo-clad figure enters the room. "Damn it, sorry, I didn't mean to . . . didn't know . . . are you hurt?" The crisp black silk of men's trousers crinkles as the offender crouches down and stretches his hand my way.

I blink. Then blink again. Wide pools the color of whiskey I've drooled over during movie nights with the girls peer at me.

"Are you okay?" An expression worthy of an Oscar nomination graces Asher Menken's face as he scans my body for broken bits.

I wiggle my toes, rub my shoulder, and swivel my head around. "All in one piece, no thanks to you." I've wanted to approach him since I first saw Ash on the red carpet a couple of feet ahead of us, but he was in the middle of an interview, probably the one I'd just been listening to. He and my big brother Owen are still best friends, but over a decade has passed since the superstar and I have been in the same room together.

"What can I do?" There is no spark of recognition in his eyes despite the fact that other than the long hair, I'm a mini copy of my brother. I wait to see if anything clicks, but his focus is not on my face. Rather, he gawks at my naked leg, exposed in all its glory thanks to the thigh-high slit in this fancy dress. His gaze travels up my leg and I follow, until we get to where the lace of my aquamarine thong is visible, no longer shielded by the Spanx. He looks at my hair, then my thong, and swallows.

"I still like matching things," I say.

"Sorry?"

"My hair matches my thong. Like my hair bows used to match my clothes, remember?"

His eyes narrow, and he tilts his head. "I think you might've hit your head."

"I'm Siobhan." I lift the sleeve off my left wrist and show him the tiny star, my very first tattoo. I got the memento as soon as I moved here seven years ago: my design, based on the one I drew for Ash a lifetime ago. "Réiltín?"

Another sweep of his eyes takes in more of my face as he scans me up and down, or left to right, or however the horizontal plane is looked at. "Owen's little sister?" His eyebrow rises.

"Aye."

"Unbelievable." He reaches inside his jacket, pulls out his wallet, and takes out a piece of paper. Ash sits next to me on the icy floor as I tug at the dress in a too-late attempt to cover up. He gives the paper to me. "My good luck charm."

I stare. In my hand is a faded copy of what I now have on my wrist. The original little star I drew for him when I was nine.

"You . . . kept this?"

Asher casts his eyes to the floor, and my pulse takes off. I mean, I've seen the expression before, both on and off the screen, yet up close and personal like this he's . . . gorgeous. Yes, the teeth are perfect, the chin is chiseled, and the hair—oh, how I want to run my hands through his hair to test if those strands are as tuggable as they appear. But this is more than the good looks. He's lit up from within.

I hand the piece of paper from the past back to him and will my heart to slow.

"Owen did say you lived here." Ash tucks the drawing carefully back in his wallet and puts it away. "Of all places to run into you." He smiles, and there's the "I'm sorry" smile that got him out of a trip to the police when he bumped into a car in front of us. The lady who owned the Peugeot let him go with, "What's one more scratch on this old heap of metal?" She would've berated any of my brothers for doing the same thing.

"I promised my friends not to get starstruck, but I didn't think they meant literally." I smile back. "Howeyeh, Ash? Can I still call you that?"

He nods, giving me the once over again. "Can't call you Little Star anymore. You're no longer . . . little."

My turn to swallow. The way he said *little* sends a shiver through me that I can't blame on the chill of the tile floor. My name is a puzzle for most people in LA. At work I heard a million attempts at my name until I came up with "she-Vaughn." Sarah shortens it to just Sio, "she." Back in Ireland my family calls me Shiv, and Mum insists on Baby Girl. But Asher's nickname for me, Réiltín, which means Little Star, might be my favorite. "I don't mind." He can call me anything.

"Réiltín it is, then." He runs his hand through the thick light brown strands he inherited from his movie star mother and rests his fingers on the nape of his neck. "We should probably get off this floor." He jumps to his feet, wraps his fingers around my wrist, and lifts me up. I wince in pain.

"Did I hurt you?"

"The shoulder is a bit tender." I lower the neckline and see a red line across my skin. Ash's thumb traces the mark from the door. His touch doesn't make the pain go away, but I'm both nervous and more secure with his skin on mine. His presence has always had this effect on me. The thrill and the comfort at the same time.

The first time I met him, my nine-year-old self didn't know what to think about Ash. He wasn't a famous Hollywood star then, just the nineteen-year-old friend my brother brought home for Christmas break because Ash had no family in Ireland to spend the holiday with. A breath of fresh air all the way from California to light up our middle-of-nowhere in County Kerry.

I fix my dress. "We should get going. My friend Sarah must be wondering where I am."

"Sure you're okay?"

"I'm tougher than I seem."

"You look"—he pauses—"great in this dress. All grown-up." His eyes stray to my cleavage.

"Yup." I straighten and push my chest forward. "Got me big girl boobs and everything."

"I didn't mean to . . ." His "I'm sorry" smile is back. "This isn't what I—"

"Just having a laugh." I tap him on the arm, like we're old pals. "Great way to start my next quarter century."

"Today?"

"'Tis."

"Well, happy birthday to you." He purses his lips, and his eyes brighten. "We could have a drink after the gala? Celebrate? Catch up?"

"Bang on." I don't jump up and down like I used to when I got to spend time with him, but I flash him my "thank you for a great tip" smile. Asher Menken wants to have drinks with me. I ain't saying no.

"Great. But"—he rubs the wrinkles between his eyebrows—"a favor? Could you check if there is a guy in a red velvet tuxedo hanging around by any chance? If he is, I'll stay here a while longer."

"Aye." I peek out of the door and see empty hallways. "The coast is clear."

★ ★ ★

Reporter 1: Did you see Asher on the red carpet tonight? No Leyla by his side.

Reporter 2: My heart broke when I heard about the demise of #AshLa.

Reporter 1: But he did look fine. Like, rebound fine. Any bets who the next lucky girl will be?

Reporter 2: One-night stand with Asher Menken? Sign me up.

Two

Asher

Siobhan Casey.

I can't believe Owen's baby sister scared my bathroom stalker off with foul language worthy of an R-rated movie. The creep thought he was clever hiding around the corner, ready to accost Siobhan and me on our way to the ceremony. Her vocabulary, among other things, has grown. In fact, there isn't much left of the little girl with a short bob, matching hair accessories, and hand-me-down outfits from her brothers. Although the eyes, those sometimes green, sometimes blue, sometimes gray eyes of hers, and Owen's, and their Ma's. I should've recognized those eyes.

When my publicist Jackson asked me to be part of tonight's ceremony, I almost said no. I hate these types of affairs. The fakeness. The shallowness. The constant vying for attention. I never dreamed my night would be like this.

I glance out into the sea of creativity, and the rush of youthful exuberance hits me like a tidal wave. My partnership with the Starlight Foundation was the right decision. This is the perfect project to kickstart my new production company. I already got the green light for two TV shows, and this movie, with the proper amount of press, will give me the cachet to do more.

Still, the best part is the opportunity to give back, do something worthwhile with the fame I've been lucky enough to achieve. And when the tall kid accepts his Best Director award, he's genuinely ecstatic. I can't help grinning like a fool along with him.

"That's Nick." Siobhan sits down after she finishes clapping her hands raw. An empty seat next to me had been an open invitation for the opportunists looking to pitch, but now I'm glad the organizers assumed I would bring a date. "He's been in LA less than six months, and look at him. I'm here seven years and keep slinging drinks."

"You want to be in the movie business?"

"God, no. Owen is the one with the acting bug in our family."

"Why LA then?" Owen refused to tell me the full story.

"Farthest place I could escape to with my American passport that met my criteria."

"Which were?"

"Far from Ireland, fun, sunny, and not an island." She winks at me. Good to see she hasn't lost her spunky attitude. "Had a string of jobs. Let's see, I was the Belgian waffle girl at Disneyland first. Girl's gotta start somewhere. Graduated to waitressing at a fifties themed diner. Gawd, that was horrible.

They put that yellow American plastic they call cheese on everything. Who puts cheese on pie?"

Siobhan has the right to judge. Her family's cheese is the best I've ever tasted. Of course, I've had the privilege of stealing the stuff fresh from the cheese fridge when no one was looking. As a teenager I preferred to ask for forgiveness rather than permission. The bonus of performing in Dublin was that in three hours I could be at the Casey farm indulging in unlimited quantities of first-rate cheese. Well, and pretending I'm part of their large warm family. Owen is so lucky.

"Anyhow, now I work at a swanky resort bartending with my girl Sarah over there"—she swings her champagne glass in the direction of a group of young people, of which Sarah could be any one of three girls—"but the hours give me time to play artist."

"Well, lucky me. You saved me from being cornered by overeager fans and wannabe writers." And she saved me before. The first Christmas I spent at her family's farm, she saw me struggle to memorize my part for *The Little Prince*. I was ready to throw in the towel. Maybe the acting gene skipped a generation, maybe the tabloids were right and my good looks and family connections were the only reasons Trinity's theatre program accepted me.

Siobhan didn't let me give up. She ran lines with me, jumped up and down every time I got one right, and even drew me a picture of a little star, a réiltín, for good luck. The folded piece of paper with her design was in my pocket when I first went on stage and has been with me ever since, calming me when I'm nervous. And being back in the States has me super nervous tonight.

"He deserved the tongue-lashing. Shoving his script at you in the middle of the event is the worst way to get your attention."

"Hollywood is hard, I get it. But he was going to stuff the flash drive inside my jacket if you didn't interfere. I should've just shoved him off, but that'd end up in the papers with me as the unreasonable superstar, too stuck-up to talk to his fans." I take another sip from the flute the server keeps refilling. "The guy's face matched his red suit after you told him off. You're more effective than my bodyguards."

She laughs. Not the polite tut-tut of reporters reacting to my lame jokes or the light tinkle that warmed my heart when I managed to get Leyla to break character. No, this is a roaring, full-bodied, full-of-life laugh.

And I'm laughing along with her, feeling lighter than I've felt in months. No, years.

My real smile hasn't graced my face in forever. The world thinks Leyla and I broke up a few weeks ago. In reality, we've been apart for over a year. Our publicists timed the news for maximum impact, every step calculated to advance our careers. Well, her career. It's always been about her career. Every fight, a tug of war between her need to shoot for the stars and mine to settle down. In the end, our marriage came down to one thing: I can't wait to have kids, and she didn't want any.

"Gotta stand up for myself and those I care about," Siobhan says. "You know my older brothers; add waitressing in LA, and there's no better verbal self-defense school." She curls her arm and almost spills champagne onto herself. I catch the glass in time. "I know how to punch, too, if it comes to it. Owen made sure to teach me. And I always keep my thumb out."

She puts her glass down and demonstrates the proper fist technique. "Brothers." Her eyes widen. "Oh." She holds out her hand. "Give me your phone. Let's send Owen a selfie. It'll freak him out."

I like nothing more than pulling pranks on my best friend. My phone in hand, Siobhan leans in, her shoulder brushing against mine, and I inhale a mixture of honey and something spicy. "Smile," she instructs.

Easily done.

She plucks my cell from my fingers, her thumbs fly over the screen, and in a second, she flashes our smiling faces at me. "Check out who I bumped into," is written underneath our picture.

"Bumped into, huh." I chuckle at her play on how we met in the bathroom. She sends the text.

Siobhan opens my jacket, the gesture she berated the guy in the red suit for. "Done."

My body shrunk away from the rando's touch, but with my grown-up réiltín, I savor the contact. She puts my phone in the inside pocket and adjusts my sky-blue tie. Her eyes narrow, and she runs her fingers against the dots on the smooth silk.

"This tie, doesn't it remind you of the *Infinity* exhibit Yayoi Kusama did with the mirrors at The Broad a few years ago?"

I nod. "Like being inside a kaleidoscope." I took Leyla on a private tour of the immersive art installation at The Broad Modern Art Museum. We spent the evening lost in the multi-reflective rooms.

"Exactly." She smooths my tie one more time. The touch of her hand on my chest does things to me it should not. "Wasn't it deadly? Blows you only got five minutes in each room."

She's deadly. Real and beautiful. And alluring.

Gone is the little girl who doodled on anything she could get her hands on. Before me sits this vivacious, gorgeous woman. Her green—or are they blue—eyes twinkle in the low light of the reception hall.

"Did you study art?"

"I take classes when I can, but nothing official. I love to explore—oils, watercolors, sculpture, loom, pottery, print—tried them all. I even thought about costume design. But I think skin is my favorite canvas." She looks down at the star on her wrist.

This woman is a bright star in the dark night that has been my life lately. I can't look away; I won't, not when there's so much to see.

Even her dress teases by covering up practically everything yet accentuating her body in a way no garment should be allowed to. But I've glimpsed the secrets the fabric hides. Thinking about her long leg and how I'd run my hand up the curves to . . . I feel a twitch I haven't felt in a long time.

What am I doing? How can I be thinking like this? What would Owen say if he saw me ogling his sister?

Hey, boyo, don't even think about touching her.

Which is exactly what I'm doing. Thinking. And that's where I'll be stopping.

"So, you've traveled the world?" Siobhan reaches for another glass from the server walking by and our hands brush.

There it is again, the little electric shock like when I touched her in the bathroom. What is she doing to me? Am I having any effect on her? It's so hard for me to tell these days, reality and fiction always blurring. Is a woman truly interested in me, or is she just caught up in my fame and fortune?

It was easy when I met Leyla. We were both unknowns at the time, just starting out in the business. When our movie hit number one at the box office everything changed overnight. I was used to my parents' fame and seeing my face on the cover of tabloids wasn't new, but with my own fame, the frenzy reached a whole different level. Leyla and I relied on each other, bonded in the fire of chaos.

Siobhan is different. She knows me and doesn't have the starstruck expression my fans get. Talking to her brings the instant comfort I associate with my visits to her family farm. She taps her glass to mine, and I enjoy another brush of our fingers.

Her skin is cool. No, comfort isn't the right word. Connection? There's something here. We're on our third glass and I should be feeling the haziness of the alcohol, but instead, everything is crystal clear. For the first time in a long time, I'm alert and aware.

Four delicate fingers brush over the back of my hand, as if she's painting me with invisible watercolors. Her pupils dilate, and I'm sure mine do too. A slender index finger wraps around my thumb and slides up, down, and up again. If I'm reading her right, my year of celibacy is ending tonight.

She touches a sensitive part at the base of my thumb. "Wanna get out of here?" Siobhan's eyes confirm her invitation.

"Yes" escapes my lips before I even think about consequences.

"Give me a minute."

As she walks away, I text my security detail to let them know I'm ready to leave and there's going to be a plus one. Hopefully, we can slip out the back door and not get noticed.

Across the room, Siobhan's talking to a short blonde in an even shorter silver dress. They hug, and my little star's walking back toward me. Her slender hips swing with the movement, glittering gold. My body reacts with more than a twitch this time.

"Where to, sir?" asks the limo driver.

"The hotel," says Siobhan.

"How'd you—"

"Know? Figured you'd be staying with your parents since you just got back. Their house is in Malibu, right? A tad too far for tonight."

She's too smart for me.

The hotel is only a short ride from the venue, and in no time we're in the underground garage. I hop out of the car hoping to open the door for Siobhan, but she's too quick for me too. Leyla would've waited, expecting a grand gesture from me in case there were any cameras around. Always a show with that woman.

This girl—woman—however, pinches my security guard's arm. "Oh, you're a tough one." The guard sticks out his chest and eyes Siobhan up and down. "Spend every day at the gym, do we?"

I feel a pang in my chest. Jealousy? I jut out my arm. "Shall we?" Siobhan slinks hers through and leans into me. My temperature rises with the contact of her warm body as we make our way to the private elevator.

The metal doors slide together and once again we're alone.

"What is it about elevators?" she asks, a hand running down my arm.

"What d'you mean?"

"They're just so damn sexy."

"You think?"

She reaches up and tugs on my tie, giving me a low, breathy, "Yes."

I'm done for. Reason, propriety, and resistance are out the window. My lips collide with hers, one hand circling her waist to pull her closer, the other finally getting to touch the soft skin of the long lean leg she's hooked over my hip. My palm travels up her thigh and cups her butt.

The sequins of her dress scratch against my thin shirt as if they are clawing to get at me. She's amazing, and so alive. Her taste, her scent, her heat invade me, send currents through my body, and light me up like no other. The twitch is now a throb.

I don't have enough hands. I need to touch more of her, but there's no way I'm letting go of this luscious ass. I tear my mouth from hers and explore her chin, her neck. I pause, pressing my lips against her pulsing artery, the thump matching my own racing heartbeat.

The soft ding of the elevator indicates we've hit my floor, but I don't want to leave our little cocoon. Siobhan has other ideas and starts backing out of the elevator, my tie still clutched in her hand. I'm happy to follow, as long as I get to keep kissing those amazing lips.

We move down the hall, and I reluctantly break the kiss. "Wait."

"What? Bored already?"

"Not in the slightest." More like alive for the first time. "My room is this way." I clutch her arm and haul her down the hallway in the opposite direction, searching for my hotel room key with my free hand. I jam the card into the reader, the light goes green, and we burst into my suite.

Before the door closes, her fingers are undoing my belt.

"Careful of the gown. It's not mine."

The first time I roll a condom on, she doesn't even take her dress off.

★ ★ ★

Guess who ordered two burgers, not one?

Burger with Fries . . . $36.95

Burger with Fries . . . $36.95

Chocolate Cake . . . $22.95

THREE

Siobhan

FOR YEARS I WENT to bed ogling the poster of Asher in my bedroom in Ireland. Now I'm in America lying in bed with the real thing. I stare at his sleeping form, my fingers itching to trace the outline of his jaw, those plump lips.

"See something you like?" He peers at me through one half-closed eye.

"Lots. I—"

Ash's lips crash against mine, and my words are lost. Unnecessary. I open my mouth and grant him access like it's the most natural thing in the world. My lungs are screaming for air by the time he pulls away.

He doesn't go far. As if he can't stay away, he presses his forehead against mine. "I'm starved. Wanna order room service?"

Wasn't expecting that. The appetizers at the Starlight Foundation Gala were enough to sop up some of the champagne in my system, not replace a dinner. "I could eat."

Ash stretches across my body and slides the remote off the bedside table. My skin alights from the brush of his arm against my ribs, and I want his mouth back on me, charting a path along my side. I bite my lip instead. On the way back, Ash kisses my shoulder, the base of my neck . . . My brain argues with other parts of me. We are not going to get any sustenance if I don't stop this. "I thought you wanted something to eat."

"I do." His words are muffled as he savors my ear lobe. With a sigh, he pushes himself up into a sitting position and turns on the TV. "Let's see what they have."

The heat of his body leaves mine. I mimic his posture and pull up the sheet, so it covers our almost-touching knees.

While he rolls through the menu, his other hand settles on my leg. His thumb grazes my thigh, and I order my brain to concentrate on the food items scrolling on the TV instead of following my urge to grab Ash's hand and put it somewhere that thumb could be of better use. Cheese pizza, ravioli, pesto risotto . . .

"How about a burger and fries. France has decadent food, but they can't do a burger like here."

The only French food I've had is quiche lorraine at the bakery Sarah buys her butter tarts from. Must be nice to have had so much French food you crave a burger. How long has Ash been in Europe? At least two years. He followed his wife. No, ex-wife. Shit, am I his rebound?

That movie star smile flashes my way, and my heart skips a beat. So, what if I am. I don't care. I'll file away my time with him, from his hand helping me off the floor in the bathroom to what we did in this bed. Everything about this night, tucked away and treasured alongside the memories of him at our farmhouse before he was famous.

"Add some chocolate cake and you got yourself a deal." I give him my most dazzling smile, because two can play that game. He stares at my lips, menu forgotten. I bring my mouth to his. "Burgers, fries, chocolate cake, and then I'm all yours," I whisper, with our noses millimeters apart. The desire in his eyes says he wants a bite of me much more than the food, but he leans back and completes the order.

The meal arrives blazingly fast. We sit cross-legged on the bed, the tray of food between us. Ash inhales the fries like there's no tomorrow, and I have to fight him for the last one. For a man who looks like he works out every day—scratch that, several times a day—watching him wolf down a burger before I start on mine brings back the teenage Ash I knew in Ireland years ago.

"I see your eating habits haven't changed much." He used to scarf Mom's meals and ask for seconds before any of my brothers finished theirs.

"I can pretend to be more civilized when I'm on display in public, but with family this is what you get." He winks and I forget to chew. "Dad enrolled me in etiquette classes when I was in middle school because he could not stand my table manners. Now imagine me, a short pimply teenager with braces in a room where I'm the only boy, surrounded by white tablecloths and a million forks and glasses, learning how to debone fish while looking cool as a cucumber."

"The latter part I can imagine, but you as a pimply youth? Impossible."

"Just wait until my mother sits you down with a stack of photo albums. You'll get to see more of my naked ass, and the array of pimples that plagued me for a couple of years in middle school." Ash runs his finger across my cheekbone, and I forget about the fries. I want his fingers to touch my salty lips, but he takes his hand away before he can get there. "I don't remember you having those. Any time I saw you, you looked like an angel."

"Angel? Mum would disagree. She thinks I was harder to raise then the boys." I lift my chin and show off my skin that Sarah thinks is flawless. "You missed my puberty years, but I'm the lucky one. Never had a problem with bad skin. My smile is a different story. I should've had braces, but that was not something we even considered." I smile wide and reveal my less-than-perfect teeth.

"So no embarrassing teenage photos of you at your Ma's place?"

"I didn't say that. Mom still drones on about my attempts at copying the latest makeup trends. I'm sure there are photos where I look like a cartoon character. Like my year 4 portrait. She won't let that one die."

"I have to see those." He laughs, and the sound is not like in his movies. It's lighter but deeper at the same time. "Next time we're in Ireland, I'll ask your Ma."

"I'm sure she'll do whatever you tell her. I'm surprised you don't know the combination to her safe. Unlike you, I'm my mother's worst nightmare. I moved on from makeup you can wash off to coloring my body with permanent images. Look at me."

He does, and there's that pull again as his eyes travel over my shoulder, under my right breast, and down. "They suit you. Everything I see when I look at you is beautiful."

"You probably say this to all your one-night stands."

He drops his smile. His gaze roams across my exposed skin, this time without the lust I've enjoyed seeing in them this evening. He's way too serious, and my skin prickles in anticipation of what he's going to say.

"I haven't done a one-night stand since I was twenty." His gaze finds mine and holds it. "I mean it when I say you're beautiful. You're so beautiful I have to touch you constantly to remind myself you're not a figment of my horny imagination."

I take his hand and place it on top of the blue cornflower tattoos on my rib. "Definitely not imaginary."

His thumb runs over the petal imprint. "Does it hurt when you get them?"

"Feck yeah."

"Why do it again if it hurts?"

"Because I love them so much. I can take pain if I know it's going to be temporary and lead to better things." After the first one, my little star celebrating my freedom, I swore I'd never get another one. The Celtic knot behind my right ear I got in a moment of weakness, of missing home. That pain was worth not caving in. "Plus, you sort of forget how much it hurts. Mum used to say women have more than one kid because they forget how much it hurts giving birth. If they remembered, we'd all be only children."

"Do you believe it?" Ash runs his finger through the leftover ketchup in little infinity loops.

"Sorta. I think if you want a kid, you'd go through any kind of pain to have one."

His finger freezes. "Do you want to have kids?"

"Absolutely. Maybe not four, like Mum, but a couple." I bop my head and point at my heart. "I'd be a cool hot Mom. The talk of the playground."

One side of his mouth hitches in a smile. "I can picture that."

"But I need to figure shit out first. My life is, well . . ."

"Like that ever happens." He licks the ketchup off his finger.

"It happened for you." I poke him in the shoulder, trying to get that smile back. I get a glimmer. "You're successful. You can have a gaggle."

"Might look that way. But money doesn't equal success. Or happiness." His serious expression returns.

I poke him in the shoulder again. "But it buys excellent chocolate cake."

"Let's hope it does." Ash takes the silver lid off the plate.

A slice of four-layered chocolate cake filled with chocolate ganache and drizzled with so much chocolate it forms a little lake on the plate is not what captures my attention. In the middle of the decadence there's a single unlit candle. A pack of matches with the hotel logo completes the still life.

"You remembered?"

"That it's your birthday? No way I could forget anything about you." He lights the candle, and in a quiet baritone starts whispering, "Happy Birthday to Réiltín." Each note lights a little candle in my chest. The heat builds until my heart is a puddle of tenderness. He ends with a breathy 'you' worthy of Marilyn Monroe and focuses on my lips.

I tear my gaze away and blow out the candle. My wish is for Ash to be my birthday present every year.

He removes the snuffed candle and digs into the top two layers with his fork. "Would you like some?"

I open my mouth to take the gooey chocolatey forkful, but he changes direction and shoves the cake into his instead.

"No way, it's mine." I lunge at the cake and snatch the plate away from him. He stabs in the direction of where the plate was, and I lower my mouth to the crest of the slice and bite the largest chunk I can out of it. I can feel the buttercream on my cheek, but I'm not letting him win.

Ash abandons the fork and brings his face to mine. He bites from the other side, chocolate icing smudging his perfect face. I fake taking another mouthful of cake and lick the goo off his skin instead. The bristles of his stubble rub against my tongue, and the combination of Ash and chocolate might be the favorite thing I've ever tasted.

I scoot closer, and the plate slides out of my hand onto Ash, coating his abs in chocolate ganache. "Oh shite. Sorry."

"The cake is good, but I prefer to eat it, not wear it." Ash pushes off the bed and places the tray on the table. "Be right back." He disappears into the bathroom, the door closing with a soft click.

I climb out of the ginormous bed, my limbs heavy with disappointment. I was hoping this was a refueling for more fun, not a goodbye treat. If I get one night with Asher Menken, I want it to last until dawn. That's hours away. I don't want to leave but I've been through this enough to know the signals. Hell, I'm usually the one doing the "bathroom time to leave" move.

Why would this time be any different? My stomach swirls and I regret the cake, but not the laughter. Nor the genuine warmth of our conversation or the ecstasy of our bodies together. He said he doesn't do one-night stands. Does it mean I'll see him again? Or was that the old Asher? Now that he's divorced, does he only want to play? Wouldn't blame him. Play is all I ever do.

I've managed to pull on my thong and silver sandals when the light from the bathroom falls on me.

"Hey." Ash leans against the doorframe. "Where do you think you're going?"

The way he's looking at me, I have an urge to cover my naked breasts. I straighten my back. "This was fun, but it's getting late."

He crosses the room. "It's not late. Unless you want to go." His fingers brush against my wrist then, circle it. His touch sends tingles to places I shouldn't think about if I want to leave this room. I don't want to leave this room. He traces the tiny tattoo again. "My little star." His whisper is like a benediction.

Ash raises my wrist to his lips and gently caresses it. Whiskey-colored irises scan my face from under long eyelashes, and my heart gallops out of my chest. He leans forward and presses soft kisses on the tattoo on my shoulder, his hands flutter at my hip, and the hotel room begins to sway.

He drops to his knees, those long fingers pulling at the string of my thong, his tongue licking the 'not easy but worth it' line of script on my hip. I place a hand against the wall to steady myself as he strips off my underwear, lifting one foot out of a sandal, then the other. As my toes hit the plush hotel room carpet, his hot lips suck on my inner thigh, and my legs begin to wobble.

I'm floating through the air. Literally. Ash throws me over his shoulder as he stands, and a giggle erupts from me at the swift motion. Then the softest sheets I've ever slept on touch my back as he returns me to our bed. I miss his warmth, his skin on mine for the moment it takes him to climb in with me, but it doesn't last long before his lips find mine. I sink my fingers into the silkiest hair in the world and pull. I'm rewarded with a moan that radiates through his lips into my core.

"Condom." He rolls onto his back, propping himself up on his elbows. "You do it."

Those intense eyes watch my every move as I tear open the foil, release the disk, and find the right side. His body stiffens as I roll it on, and a delicious thought enters my mind. I lean down and kiss his hip. My name escapes his lips in a low moan. My tongue finds his abs, and they taste better than the chocolate cake. His fingers thread through my hair, and I sense his desperation. I feel it too. I find his lips, and he wastes no time as his body covers mine.

We fall out of time and space. Just Ash and I, together, as one.

Unlike our first or second time, everything is slow and sweet. Small movements cause ripples of pleasure I never thought possible. His fingers thread through mine, and the grip is anything but gentle, like he's afraid I might float away. I squeeze back, silently telling him I'm not going anywhere. I don't want to be anywhere but right here.

For once I'm not chasing the next high. Being with Asher is the high I want to ride forever.

★ ★ ★

Hey, hey, ladies. If you had your eye on Asher Menken, you might have to stand in line. Coming up after the break, an exclusive steamy video of him and the mystery woman everyone's talking about. Has Leyla been replaced? You won't want to miss this.

Four

Asher

An incessant buzzing wakes me. My phone won't stop ringing. I ignore the interruption and reach for Siobhan, hoping we can use the last condom in the four pack I found by the minibar last night. They really do think of everything at this hotel. My hand hits the Egyptian cotton. I try again. Nothing. I crack an eye open. The bed is empty.

More buzzing. I lift my head and scan the room. No teal-haired goddess in sight. The golden dress is gone too. I distinctly remember laying the garment across the couch after I stripped her last night, revealing the intricate designs on her body. Black and blue lines I ran my tongue along. My favorite was the little star on the pulsing veins at her wrist. Or maybe the dreamcatcher design on her thigh?

I grab the phone and see the image of my best friend. Guilt rolls in my gut as I answer.

"Hey." My voice is raspy from sleep.

"Tell me you didn't fuck my sister."

"Owen, it—"

"Shit, you did. You arse."

"Wait, how do you know about . . ." I take a breath, not wanting to finish the sentence. Just one thought of what we did in our last round in this bed, and I'm getting hard again.

"There are pictures of you two entering the hotel, but it's nothing compared to the security video. It's everywhere. You're practically shagging some mystery woman in the elevator. You can't tell, but I recognize the dress from your text, you fecking eejit. Nice to see my sister rock the green hair."

Her hair was teal, but I don't correct Owen. I switch screens and enter my name into the search engine. I hate this. I hate how the press ruins everything.

A headline reading "Asher Out with Mystery Woman" pops up. I tap the link, and I'm hit with a stunning photo of the two of us. Her head on my shoulder, her face covered by a wave of teal hair, a blast of life in the otherwise colorless picture. Her pale skin, my black tuxedo, and the black limo behind us, the gray concrete of the hotel parking structure. Seeing the way I stare at her, a huge genuine smile on my face, something unrolls inside me.

The copy is basic nonsense, and it's clear the reporter knows nothing. At least the Starlight Foundation gets a mention in the top third. My eyes catch the frozen screen of the video. Siobhan's back is to the camera, and my head is buried in her chest. The image is gray and grainy. My finger shakes as I hit play.

The clip is only eight seconds long. I bet there's a bidding war going on for the longer version. I need to call my publicist right away and instruct Jackson to buy the original so I can squash this. But first, I need to make things right with my best friend. And then I need to find Siobhan. How do I do that?

"When I told you to reach out when you got home, I did not mean shag her."

"Does this mean I'm no longer your best man?" The one thing I've been looking forward to these last six months is Owen and Teresa's wedding. Standing beside my friend at such an important and joyful time means the world to me.

"Not looking good."

"What if I said it just kind of . . . happened?" I recognize how lame my excuse is.

"Well, it ain't happening again. Stay away from her."

Kat: So, Sal, where is Asher spending Christmas? That's the question on everyone's lips. The man's been suspiciously absent. Is there a secret rendezvous with Leyla to blame? Are they getting back together? Or does his disappearance involve that mystery woman with the, ahem, colorful hair, who's vanished?

Sal: I don't know, Kat, but I'd put my money on him holed up in some small town "cuddling" someone.

FIVE

Siobhan

"ARE YE GRAND?" I ask the tiny image of Sarah's face in the corner of my screen as she admires the view out of my childhood bedroom. The wet winter chill nips at my skin even through the wooly sweater Mum left in my room. The sleet does not a white Christmas make. I remember at most five times we had snow on or around Christmas on the farm. This is just rainy and gray. "Enough quaint Irish winter for you? Can I close the window now?"

I turn click on the flip button on my phone. Sarah's face fills the screen. My usually-smiling roommate is also decked out in a sweater, except hers is blue with a white maple leaf plastered across her chest. I've seen the logo far too many times since living with Sarah and know either there's a hockey game tonight, or she's moping. Blond hair piled on top of her head in a messy bun makes me pick moping.

"It's so pastoral. Not the dull gray of Toronto this morning. Neither of us gets a white Christmas this year." The bottom of a cup obscures Sarah's face as she drains her first coffee of the day and pads back into her parents' kitchen for a refill. "Hoped a chat with my bestie would perk me up, but you're grumpier than I am. I blame mine on the bartender who kicked me and my three Girlsketeers out at two a.m."

"Girlsketeers?"

"Yeah, like the three musketeers, but they're girls."

"Oh cute. Can I be one?"

"Anytime you're bar hopping with us in Toronto, you're the fourth for sure." She stifles a yawn. "You have to promise to take me to the best pubs when I visit Ireland."

"Wasn't planning on coming back here any time soon." Or ever. This trip was required. Mum would disown me if I missed my brother's wedding. "The bank account won't stay in the black if I keep buying plane tickets. I'm supposed to be saving, not spending on getting you gargled."

"You know I got you. Your goals are more important than my fantasy of a *wee nip* of all the famous Irish whiskeys in their homeland."

I close the window and plunk down on the twin bed hogging two-thirds of my childhood room in the attic of the farmhouse. Try as I might, it's impossible to avoid the poster of Asher from his first romantic movie staring at me from the wall.

"What's in that head of yours and what are you staring at?" Sarah asks when a lull enters our chat. I flip to the back camera on my phone and show her the bright smile. A reminder of the night I can't forget, no matter how much I try.

"Why haven't you taken it down?"

"Stupid thing's glued to the wallpaper. I don't want to deface this room." Not like I haven't thought about it. The idea of doing something to his perfect face first visited me the week after I spent the night in his bed. I thought he'd call or text or send me a surprise bouquet of flowers, but silence was the only thing I received from Mr. Perfect. Sarah shot down my plan to show up on his parents' doorstep to punch him in the teeth. Tearing his smug face off the wall would bring so much satisfaction. "Besides, Mum adores him. Thinks he walks on water. She'd be suspicious." And I refuse to give him power over me.

"You're thinking about your night together again, aren't you?"

The glowing stop lights of my cheeks I see on the screen betray me. "It's bloody hot in here," is my non-answer.

"Take off the sweater. That would help." Sarah's suggestion is excellent, except the great wooly thing is hiding my tattoos, and if my mum saw them, let's just say baby Jesus would have to cover his ears.

To say my family isn't supportive of my artwork is an understatement. Mum thinks I only have the one on my wrist. According to her the ink is an abomination, and Da agrees with anything Mum says. I get their perspective. Tattoos aren't for everyone, but I love them. The designs offer another way to express myself.

Ash sure looked like a kid in a candy store when he first saw them the night of the Starlight Gala. His tongue seemed to enjoy tracing each one. I grow hotter at the memory. Guess they scared him off: too much for Mr. Perfect and his flawless image. I didn't fit into his world, just his bed.

"Brendan, you need trousers to go downstairs." I hear my brother Quinn run after his eldest child down the stairs.

"Men suck." On the screen in front of me, Sarah winces. Neither of us want to talk about the men in our lives. Or not in our lives. "Still, this might be your opportunity to give him a piece of your mind. Get him out of your system."

"Unlikely." It's like Ash ruined other men for me. Before him, I had no problem with love 'em and leave 'em. Ever since our hotel shagfest, I get started but can't close the deal with anyone. There's no spark.

"New topic." Sarah slams her hand on the arm of the chair she's perched on. "How's being back under your mom's roof?"

"We're both being very . . . considerate." Not a quality I tend to possess. "The whole business is bloody infuriating."

Strained relationships with our mothers is one of the many things Sarah and I have in common: only girl, unruly brothers, parents who had plans for our future. We also both escaped our childhood homes for sunny LA. Difference is, she told her family about her runaway plans. I, on the other hand, packed up for college, kissed Mum and Da goodbye, bypassed the dormitory waiting for me in Dublin, and headed straight for the airport. Called Owen once I landed in LA and begged him to tell the family what I'd done and that I wasn't coming home.

There's a clatter of pots and pans from two floors below. "I best crack on. Ma's fussing downstairs to make everything perfect for you-know-who."

"Give the fam my love," says Sarah, and we sign off. She's never met any of them, but it's like my friend's part of the family since she's been on so many video calls with me back in LA.

Sarah is the sister I've always wanted. As a kid, I used to beg my mum to have another baby. At the time I couldn't understand why she refused. Now I get the poor woman was done after four boys.

The unplanned accident known as me happened when Da and Mum celebrated New Year's a bit too hard. In Canada for a year on an all-expense-paid exchange program among cheese farmers, they finally had some cash to whoop it up. They came back to Ireland with enough money to expand and modernize the farm and a little bonus. Me. Their "last weekend in North America babymoon to Chicago without the boys" turned into a day of Mum being rushed to Chicago Medical, where I was born in the cab before she got a chance to get in the door.

"Brendan! Get your arse back down here."

I peek out the door and get an eyeful of Brendan's naked bottom. The toddler giggles and runs back down the stairs, an activity I was forbidden as a child. My older brother's little munchkins rule Mum's heart, and she lets them do whatever they please when they stay over. I understand her feelings. I seriously adore them. Watching Brendan and Kelley open presents on Christmas morn almost had me consider moving back to this middle-of-nowhere town. I follow the little rascal down to the ground floor, where my brother catches him and wrangles white underwear with Paw Patrol dogs onto him.

The third step from the bottom squeaks as I hit the worn wood. Nothing ever changes here. Mum comes barreling out of the kitchen, dish towel over her shoulder, potato in one hand, peeler in the other. "Baby Girl, there you are. I need help. I'm making Asher's favorite." Of course she is.

For some reason Mum decided Ash needed a second mother, an Irish one. From the moment he stepped into our living room years ago, she's treated Ash like the superstar he turned out to be. I couldn't get her to go to the shops in Dublin for a girls' day out, but she was first in line opening night for any of his movies. Didn't mind telling the town all about him either. Sometimes I think she likes Ash better than her own sons.

"I thought I'd pop into town and pick up some blood sausage for breakfast." The promise of picking up another Ash favorite should get me out of cooking and delay the inevitable embarrassing reunion. Believe me, I've racked my brain to find a way to avoid Ash this weekend. But seeing as we're both in the wedding party, he as best man, me as fourth bridesmaid to the right after Teresa's three sisters, I'm going to have to face him.

There's a chance he won't recognize me.

After the "event," I dyed my hair deep blue, both as a sign of solidarity for my girl Sarah's movie "*Indigo*" and in an attempt not to be recognized as the mystery woman who mounted the great Asher Menken in a hotel elevator. Worked like a charm. No one knows it was me except Sarah and Owen. And Mr. Perfect, of course.

He ignored the note with my phone number that I left by the sink in his bathroom. I should've woken him up instead of tiptoeing out of his room in an attempt to be on time for my morning shift at the resort. To add insult to injury, the pretentious pretty boy chose to stand me up at the coffee shop

Owen arranged for Ash to meet me at so we could clear the air. Didn't even have the decency to tell me face-to-face he wasn't interested in taking things beyond our one time together.

Speak of the devils. The door swings open, and in walks Owen and Ash. Just my luck. Ash wipes the slush off his peacoat and shakes his head. My below-the-navel zone clenches, as if months haven't passed since Ash had anything to do with it. He's not even here five minutes and neglected parts of my body decide to come alive. Cop yourself on!

"Asher, darlin', you're here." Mum shoves Owen aside and engulfs the movie star. A warmth of a different kind spreads through my chest as I watch him close his eyes and give in to the hug. He gets points for that. Ash is genuine with my folks.

"Ma Casey. So good to be here."

Mum releases him. "Let me get a good look at you." She pushes Ash's sopping wet hair from his forehead. The move reminds me of playing with his hair as he obsessed over the lavender tattoo under my right breast in the hotel bed. Heat flares on my cheeks. Mum grabs his chin and turns his face this way and that, tutting away. With the second swivel our eyes meet.

"Hey, Little Star,"

Blast. I'm in trouble.

★ ★ ★

Our favorite nice guy, Asher Menken, has indeed been spotted at Dublin International Airport's arrival gates. Fans are speculating if he's back to Europe for good. Is he on his way to Barcelona where Leyla was spotted earlier this week, or is he escaping the palm trees for a new secret project? Whatever his plans are, we all wish we looked this good after a ten-hour flight. Oh, wait, a private jet might help us mere mortals achieve that level of perfection too.

Six

Asher

"I booked a hotel," I say. Owen steers the car through the maze of roads out of the airport. The Finn Harps baseball cap I gave him last year for Christmas covers his muddy brown hair. Feels weird to be sitting in the front left seat and not be the one driving. I've missed this.

"Unbook it," he says. We lean right as he careens around a corner.

"Where d'you propose I sleep?"

"My room, where else? You can take the top bunk."

"Are you listening to yourself? I can rent every room at the hotel, and you want me to share a bunk bed with you?"

"You always stay with us. And I'm not sleeping in the same room with Shiv."

"And how am I supposed to be in the same house as your sister?"

"Mum'll kill me before me own wedding if you don't stay at the farm. You, she'll smile at, and I'll get the thrashing." Owen changes lanes like we're in a car chase.

"It'll be weird. Since . . . well . . ." I'm not saying since I've had sex with her. Never had a problem talking about my girlfriends with Owen before Leyla and I got hitched. Maybe I'm out of practice. Or maybe his sister is not and will never be my girlfriend.

"Things'll only be weird if you make it so. You insisted she was an adult and could make her own choices. Well, she chose not to see you again. Deal with your raging libido." The car speeds up, well past the limit, I'm sure. "If you don't start any eye fucking, which under Mum's roof isn't a good idea at the best of times, you should be fine. I don't think Shiv's interested."

"I can't blame her." I absorb the rolling not-so-green hills. Siobhan's silence after Owen passed her my contact info was a clear sign she wasn't interested in being blasted across the tabloids. Fame comes with strings attached.

Everyone in the world wants to be seen with you, but no one wants to just be with you. One of the reasons I love hanging with my best buddy and his family. Their little farmhouse in the middle of nowhere is a slice of heaven. When things cooled between Leyla and me, I knew the Caseys would take me in.

The white house appears, and Owen parks at the bottom of the driveway behind four other vehicles. A downpour of icy water starts the moment I open the car's door. We make a mad dash to the covered porch, but the trip is long enough to soak me all the way through. I don't remember the last time my underwear was wet from the rain.

The moment I enter the house I'm enveloped in an unrestrained hug. My parents are great. I love them, and they love me. Still, there's nothing like a hug from Owen's mother. I bet it's because she has so many kids. As an only child I've always been envious of Owen's big family. I wanted to make one just like his with Leyla. She didn't.

I open my eyes, and the girl I've been dreaming about stands two feet away staring at me, as stunning as she was the night she left me starstruck. Siobhan's darker, almost navy-blue hair is piled on top of her head. Her chameleon eyes match the color of the darkening stormy night outside, complete with angry clouds and a possibility of lightning. I shift in Ma Casey's tight hug. At least this woman loves me, and the love of one Casey woman should be enough.

Siobhan and I are adults; we can be civil with each other. I've never had an issue talking to women after we went our separate ways. I look back at the blue-haired beauty. "Hello, Little Star."

Her eyes narrow; she gives me the middle finger, which Owen behind me surely saw as well, and storms through the door to the left. Ah, the kitchen, the magical place where Ma Casey makes potatoes taste like the elixir of Gods.

"You're drenched, son. Shift yourself to the shower. Owen'll fetch your things." She shoos an equally waterlogged Owen out into the rain with one hand while pushing me to the stairs. "I put new fluffy towels in the guest bath. Those are yours. Leave the raggedy ones for Owen. He's used to them."

I snicker at my friend, who throws me a glare and slams the front door behind him.

This alone might be worth a night on the bunk bed. I'll sweet-talk Ma Casey into letting me take the whole family over to the hotel tomorrow. I'll get Jackson to book the entire place and my second mom can enjoy a couple of days in a suite with a jet tub. What better way to pay for years of their hospitality *and* get a room to myself?

After the hot shower I take a white shirt and dark jeans out of the suitcase Owen dragged up two flights of stairs to the attic. His is one of the two rooms under the eaves of the house, and the place is sweltering. Bet Ma Casey has the heat turned on high for me. I roll up my sleeves and rush barefoot down the well-used staircase. The third step from the bottom squeaks as I hit the worn wood. Thank goodness they haven't fixed it. The steadiness and stability of this place erases my worries, like I am in a different universe. When I'm here, I can let my guard down and be the Ash only my parents and real friends get to meet. The Casey family *is* my family.

The kitchen is bursting with a gap-toothed and pants-less Brendan and toddler Kelley dressed in her reindeer onesie performing a song I don't recognize, using the large pot for their drum and other kitchenware for pretend instruments. Brendan drops the wooden spoon he was banging with and hugs my knees so tight I lose my balance for a second.

"Unki Ashi," screams Kelley, jumping up and down, making more noise than the jam session I interrupted.

"Let go of him." Ma Casey peels Brendan off me. "Sit down. I'm sure between the flight and the drive here you must be exhausted. Dinner will be ready soon, and I'm making your favorite, Dublin coddle with an extra side of champ."

She pushes me onto a wooden chair at the table next to Siobhan, three peeled potatoes, and a mountain of unpeeled ones.

"I'm going to make you a cuppa to warm you up." Ma Casey busies herself at the stove. The kitchen is hotter than the attic, and I'm not sure hot tea is something I want or need, but I'm not suicidal. No one says no to an offer of tea in this household.

"That would be great, thanks, I love your tea," I say with a smile.

"Kiss ass," Siobhan mutters under her breath, loud enough for me but not her mom to hear.

"Good evening to you, too, Little Star." I don't mean to tease her, but the nickname seems to piss her off more than it should bother someone with no feelings toward me. She raises her eyebrows and burns me with her death stare. One eerily similar to the gaze of doom I've seen Ma Casey give her brothers Owen, Quinn, Daniel, and Jacob, but this is the first time I find myself the receiver of one. Beads of sweat on her forehead make the evil eye a little less scary.

My gaze falls to the oversized sweater she's wearing. The monstrosity would be appropriate if we were walking through a blizzard but looks ridiculously uncomfortable in the sweltering heat of this kitchen.

"Are you naked under the sweater, or is there a reason you're baking over there?" I whisper to her out of the corner of my mouth, watching Ma Casey's machinations at the stove.

"None of your beeswax," Siobhan whispers.

"I thought you were a grown-up. My mistake." The image of her very adult naked body sprawled beneath me as I kissed my way over her tattoos flashes in my mind. I grab the back of my neck and squeeze. Siobhan has the body of a woman, but she's still ten years younger than me, a baby. Always will be.

"Sure, Mr. Perfect. Bang 'em and forget 'em is such a mature stance. Or is your brief attention meant to be a gift to us simple folk?"

I rotate her way. "What are you talking about?"

"Pffft." She repeats her death stare. "You forget I actually know you. So, your fake innocence act won't work here."

Is she talking about something I'm supposed to understand?

"Here's your tea, luv." Ma Casey sets a steaming cup of tea in front of me. "The rain let up. I'll dash to the cheese shed to get us some for dinner. Ask Baby Girl here to get you anything else you might need." The kitchen door bangs with her exit, and it's me, Siobhan, and the little musicians singing into their spoon microphones and dancing around the table.

I twist my body toward Siobhan and rest my hand on hers before she can pick up a new potato. "Tell me what you're so angry at me about."

Welcome back to Entertainment Now. We're counting down our top twenty shocking moments of the year. In at number five is Asher Menken and his short, too short, sizzling elevator make-out session with a teal-haired woman in a gold sequin dress. We're still looking for any information on who this harpie is. But should we care? Was their reel a one-night-only showing? We miss AshLa! Can't our favorite *it* couple get back together and make our hearts swoon again?

SEVEN

Siobhan

I CAN'T TAKE THIS. His hand on mine is the final drop in the gradual but inevitable overheat. The irritation with the sweater, the need to hide my tattoos and pretend to be someone I'm not with my own family, the condescending look of concern on Ash's face, like I'm an oversensitive woman who can't appreciate a one-night stand for what it's worth—the pressure combusts inside me.

"Mamma," screams Kelley as she runs into the hall, Brendan in tow.

"Thank all that's good and great in this world, you're back," Quinn hollers at Caitriona, his wife, who's just walked in the door.

I can't hold irritation in. I lean toward Ash. "I'd have to care about you first to be angry."

My words are mean on purpose, because I don't want him to know how much I bleedin' care. How much he hurt me, how many sleepless nights he caused, and how he screwed up my chances with other men. That no matter how much I feign I don't think about him, it's actually all I do.

Not like he ever thinks of me. Good enough for a shag but not to be seen with. Was I too wild for him? Too forward? Too many instructions on what I like and how to touch me? Should I have hidden myself with him and pretended anything he does is ideal, instead of asking for what I wanted? Stroking egos is not part of my portfolio.

Were my parents right? Should I have stayed here? Stayed humble? My job as a bartender in LA isn't any different from anything I can find at the local pub. If I'd stayed, followed the rules, played the demure daughter role, I'd not be the black sheep of the family, the one everyone gossips about. I'd fit in.

"Then what are you not angry with me about, my Little Star?" His words are like honey as he runs his thumb over my knuckles. That's my move. I jump off the chair, sending the piece of furniture flying on its side across the kitchen floor.

"I am *not* a little anything, and I most definitely am not *yours*. Don't think you can come in here and sweet talk me into sleeping with you again. I don't repeat my mistakes. I'm smarter than you give me credit for. Fuck off and find yourself another Irish bedwarmer."

I throw the potato peeler on the table, but the blade bounces and hits Ash's hand, the one that a moment ago sent electricity through me. A bright red spot appears on his thumb, and my first instinct is to rush back to him, to offer help, to put a sticky plaster on and kiss his pain away. Instead, I grit my teeth and run out of the room, colliding with Owen, who's dragging another bucket of potatoes from our root cellar. Or was. The impact causes the bucket to drop and pale brown pratties spill all over.

"Hot potata!" cries Brendan. The kids scramble between our legs, picking them up and throwing them back into the bucket. Each one clangs against the metal of the pail in a rhythm matching the staccato of my racing heart.

Owen pinches my elbow and drags me out of the kitchen and into the hollow under the stairs, while Ash, after almost falling over the potato minefield, helps the kids collect the vegetables off the floor. "Quick kids, before they get cold."

"Tell me I did not just hear the F word come out of your mouth?" His breath is hot on my cheek. "When you're in this house, Mum's house, you play the nice daughter and leave your wild Hollywood bollocks in LA. How hard is it to be a normal person for a week? A week. That's all I asked for. Then you can go back to your foolin'."

His fingers dig into me, and I lean away from him, leaving him holding part of my sleeve. The wool of my sweater stretches, and the tattoo of the lotus on my shoulder slides into view.

"For fuck's sake." Owen lets go of me and tugs the neckline back up. "Did you get more? Cover yourself."

A cool breeze hits me, followed by Mum as she walks in carrying a crate filled with cheese. "Jesus, Mary, and Joseph, what's all this now? Why's everyone in the entryway? Asher, dear, whatever are you doing on the floor? Let me get those."

Over my shoulder I see Ash, and his face lacks the smile we all have come to expect. Whiskey-stained eyes bore into me and Owen.

"All done, Ma. No problem." Ash rubs the back of his neck and gives Mum a half-hearted smile. "I need a word with Owen."

"Oh, of course, you boys go talk. Baby Girl and I will finish with the potatoes and get the table set." Mum shakes her hand for me to clear the way through for Ash.

I bound several steps up the stairs and stop on the one that squeaks. "Give me a tik, Mum. I need to pop to my room. This sweater's making me itch." I don't wait for her reply, running up two steps at a time, and slam the door to my bedroom shut. I peel the sweater off, ball the wretched thing, and throw it on the floor.

There's no thump, no release of the fury inside me. Young Ash smiles at me from the wall, and I can't take his stupid grin anymore. I grip a corner and rip the poster off. The damned thing comes off in one clean sheet: unmarred, smooth, and ready to be hung again. The gall. Even in paper form I have no effect on Mr. Perfect. I let the poster fall on the carpet by my bed.

Down on my knees, I slide my suitcase from under the bed, rifle through my clothes, and find a yellow long-sleeved T-shirt with a bright pink and green lotus. The design is mine, a copy of the one I drew for my shoulder, but this one has a bit more color. My family might not approve of the art on my skin, but they can't complain about this version. Time they got used to the idea of me being an artist.

Outside my room, I pause when I hear voices coming from behind the closed door of Owen's room. I tiptoe closer.

"I lied." Owen's voice is hushed and soft. "I never gave her your number. I told Shiv you'd meet her for coffee and neglected to tell you about the agreement, so she'd think you stood her up."

Ash's voice booms through the house. "You did what?"

He did what? My pulse races, and I step closer.

There's a loud thud. Did Ash hit Owen? My hand is on the doorknob, ready to defend my thick, lying brother.

"Is it because you think I'm not good enough for her?" Ash doesn't sound like himself, the confidence from the kitchen gone.

"Ah, don't be a bleedin' eejit. You know I think you're grand." I can almost see Owen making a face at Ash. "The movie star malarky is bollocks. You're one of the most genuine people I know. I'd be lucky to call you my actual brother."

"Then why?"

Yeah, why?

"It's your world, man. I don't want her to get caught up in that paparazzi shit." Owen pauses, and I bite the inside of my cheek, anxious for more. "I saw how they treated Leyla, judged her, ripped her apart over a simple fashion choice. They'd eat Shiv alive."

"Don't you think that should be her choice?"

Points for Ash.

"I know, I know. But she's my little sister. It's my job to protect her."

"She's a strong independent woman who, from what I've seen, can handle herself quite well."

More points for Ash.

"I don't want to think about what you've seen."

Something falls, and I think I hear punches. If anyone should be punching these two muppets, it's me. I push the door open and the painted panel hits Ash's back. Owen's fist freezes in the air inches from my face. I take a step inside his room and slap my big brother's cheek while holding my finger to my lips. Don't need Mum running up the stairs to investigate the noise.

"You can slap me too." Ash is trying to close his shirt, which is currently missing two top buttons. "Or punch. Or kick. Whatever you need. I should've listened to my gut. Found you like I wanted. I messed up."

He wanted to find me. Wanted me. Wanted more. My chest tightens.

Ash's eyes glisten, and his lips press into a thin line. "Can we at least talk?"

"No." I grab him by the shirt collar, wipe the tension off his mouth with mine, and release the desire I've been holding on to for months. We talk with our tongues. Words would take too much time, and I've waited long enough. I show him what I want and give permission for more.

"Siobhan," Owen squawks in my ear. "Get off him."

Ash ignores my brother and accepts my invitation. With enthusiasm. We struggle for purchase on each other, our kiss a battleground. My back hits the door, and I win when I eliminate the remaining gap between our bodies. I surrender when his hands dive into my hair, tilt my head, and scorch me with the intensity of . . . everything. This heat I don't mind. Not. One. Bit.

"Leave it out." My brother keeps trying to separate us.

With a whimper, I lose Ash's lips. He whips round and punches my brother in the shoulder.

"I love you, man." Ash pushes Owen away. "But this doesn't concern you anymore. We're adults. We can do whatever we want. Stop trying to micromanage everyone."

"Micromanage. Micromanage?" My brother sinks onto the lower bunk, buries his head in his hands and I think for a moment he's laughing. No. A rapid intake of air followed by a loud sob dispels any illusion. My oldest brother, the rock, the one with all the answers, who keeps the rest of the siblings in check, who dried my tears a million times but never shed one himself, is weeping in front of me on his childhood bed.

Ash and I take the three steps separating the door from the bunkbed. I sit down next to Owen and hug him with one arm. Ash on the other side pats my brother's hunched back.

"I've messed it all up," he says through his fingers. "Mum hates me moving to Dublin. But Teresa got several offers in the capital. We've tried living apart, and the distance almost killed our relationship. I wouldn't wish this on my little sister. I didn't want you to make the same mistakes as me."

"I had no idea." I put my head on Owen's shoulder, and he wipes his eyes with his hands. "You can talk to me, you know. I'm a decent listener."

"Don't tell anyone you saw me cry. It'll ruin my reputation." So like Owen to worry about what other people think.

"Shiv," Mum hollers from downstairs. "These potatoes aren't going to peel themselves."

"We best go." Owen sniffles and wipes his cheeks with the material of his sleeve.

"Um, I need to change first." Ash points to his ruined white shirt.

"I'll lend a hand." I find Ash's fingers on the bed and cover them with mine. I can help him change, and we can squeeze in a couple of those sizzling kisses before we go down.

"Quick change and straight downstairs," says Owen, "or Mum'll be up here dragging you down by the ear."

"You can save the warning. I'm not about to make Ma Casey angry." Ash bumps his knee against mine. "Not when I want her to approve my dating her daughter."

"Date? Me?" I lift my chin higher. Did I just hear him right? Is he slagging me?

"Do you have a sister I'm not aware of?" Ash's eyes twinkle.

I move closer and land a light kiss on his lips. "You couldn't handle more than one of us." My heart is singing. Asher Menken wants to be with me enough to brave Mum's wrath. He's known the adult me for less than two days: the fastest anyone's ever committed to me. Or the slowest, if you count the three months between those two days. Either way, this is a record.

"Don't you dare bring up anything about dating before the wedding." Owen dims the joy I see in Ash's eyes. "One thing at a time. Although I'd love to witness your fall from grace and regain my title as the good son. Wait until Teresa and I are out of earshot before you break the news and take the attention for yourself."

My worry for Owen lessens. If he's giving out orders and joking again, he's going to be okay.

MediaBusters.com offers minimum of $2000 for photo and current location of Asher Menken. Email: tips@mediabusters.com

EIGHT

Asher

UNTIL I MET THE Casey family, sushi was my favorite food. LA sushi is only outmatched by the real deal in Japan. After spending four years in Ireland, my answer to "what's your favorite dish" is always Dublin coddle. Potatoes are a food group of their own I could eat exclusively. My dietitian insisted I keep the overconsumption of those to special occasions only. Hollywood doesn't want love handles on a romantic lead. But any visit to the farm is a special occasion. Today is the first time in my life I'm not enjoying Ma Casey's potatoes like I normally would. No potato extravaganza is worth prying myself from Siobhan's lips.

Eat. Smile for a bit, then head up, so I can sneak into Siobhan's room and spend the night reacquainting myself with the body parts below her chin.

"Asher, son, you're not eating." Ma Casey must've been counting every spoonful touching my lips. "Eat up. You can stand to gain some weight. Never seen you thinner."

The first projects of my production company with the Starlight Foundation winners consumed my time, so workouts and proper nutrition took the back seat. I wasted my spare time pining for the teal-haired girl I thought I had no right to pine for. Now I do. "Jetlag. I'll do better tomorrow."

"Don't you worry. I'll put the coddle away in the container with the yellow lid. You can come in the middle of the night and have some if you want."

Owen mouths something at me. I choose not to pay attention to his jabs, because I don't care what Owen thinks about me after what he pulled off. What Siobhan thinks interests me a ton. If she's thinking what I'm thinking, the night in her bedroom will not help with my jetlag.

"Put the dishes by the sink and scat. Baby Girl and I'll wash up."

Siobhan looks at me with a terrified expression. This will delay our plans for meeting up in her room.

"Let me help. The least I can do to appreciate your hospitality." I pick up my plate and the serving dish in front of me and carry them to the stack of dirty ones the rest of the family cleared before they hurried out of the kitchen like a pack of stray dogs.

"Not in this household. You're a guest. Put your feet up by the fire, watch some telly, take a nap, but you're not touching the slop."

I put my hand on Ma Casey's shoulder and snatch the frayed drying towel clashing against her starched white blouse. "How about you two wash and I dry. I'm great at it." I smile my fanciest smile at Owen's mother and watch her melt. She's so easy to sway. Telling her about me dating Siobhan will be a piece of cake. My second mother loves me too much to not be happy for us.

"You coming?" Owen shouts from the doorway. The rugby and whiskey tradition with the guys is hard to pass up, but I'm camp Siobhan today. And tomorrow. And hopefully many more days and months to come. Rugby and whiskey can wait.

"Nope. Gotta earn my scout points." Owen's eyes swivel between his sister and the sink. For a moment I think he's going to pitch in. Siobhan runs a metal brush against the sides of the giant pot responsible for the goodness we demolished during the longest family meal known to man.

My best friend pats the frame of the door. "Your loss."

"Your work's been good, then?" Ma Casey passes me a plate, and I run the towel across the shiny surface before she hands me the next one.

"Perfect. Busy. Exciting."

"Not too busy to come visit us again next year?"

"That's the plan. My Casey farm vacations are sacred." I add the dry dish to the stack of clean ones and catch another. "Jackson knows not to mess with my Christmas in Ireland. The week is already booked in my calendar, and my plans are unmovable."

"That's what I like to hear. You'll get your room back because Baby Girl's not coming for seven more years, if she avoids us again."

Next time we'll be staying at the hotel together, but this is not the time to announce my intentions. I'll get my chance.

Siobhan shoves silverware into the soapy water and reaches for a cloth. I catch her eye in the glass of the kitchen window. "I can always stay at the hotel." I tear my gaze from Siobhan and meet Ma's eye. "I wanted to talk to you about it, actually."

"Nonsense. No need to waste money when we have plenty of room here. And if you and Leyla get back together, and she decides to finally come meet us, Da and I will give you our master. We can manage."

Not getting into the Leyla conversation. That ship has sailed. We are not the on-again-off-again couple our publicists are trying to portray to keep the media interested. We're off. No amount of therapy can heal the differences in what we wanted out of our marriage.

"I mean this weekend. I thought my gift to the bride and groom could be renting out the entire Coachman's Hotel and Spa the night of the wedding. This way everyone gets to stay there and sleep the night off." I was at Quinn and Catriona's wedding, and I know there will not be many people left standing. Ma Casey knows this, too. Da will be among the people who'll need a good night's sleep next to the venue.

Ma Casey purses her lips. "That sounds expensive."

"I can afford this. If not for my best friend and my favorite family, then for whom? You only get married once." Twice for me.

"What would I do with the house? I have to be back here to feed the animals."

"I'm sure you can find a hand who can stay the night and do that for you. Especially on the day of your son's wedding." I take a dripping pan from her hand.

"That's not what I've planned."

I tap her elbow with mine. "But it's a good idea."

"Not driving late at night would be good. And I can get a nightcap myself."

She's almost convinced. "And they have a spa you can use."

"Spa. That's for the LA types. Never been to one and not planning on going to."

"A jacuzzi tub in your room?"

"That sounds mighty nice."

I wrap my arms around her and squeeze. "It's settled. I'll call Jackson and get things all sorted."

"Thanks, luv. I know money for you is different than it is for us, but the thought is what counts. You take care of me better than my own children." She nudges my chin. "Children don't come to us only by blood. You're mine, and I'm going to be your ma till the day I leave this earth. You're my child in here"—she taps the spot above her chest—"where it most counts."

Siobhan and I escape the kitchen once every pot, glass, fork, and surface is clean, dry, and spotless.

"Bang-up job talking my mum into staying at the hotel. She'd never agree if I were to ask. Owen, maybe. But you? You need to ask her what the combination to the safe is."

"She has a safe?" We evade the living room with the present-free but overly decorated Christmas tree. The men are busy drinking and watching rugby on the giant flatscreen, a recent addition to the otherwise unchanged space.

"That's where the family heirlooms are stashed."

We pause over the third step, hop over it, and giggle. I love how we share the secrets of this house. Finding out Siobhan's secrets is what I crave.

I forgot her room is even smaller than Owen's, with barely enough wall space for me to push her against. Months of yearning to touch her wash away my reserve, and within seconds her shirt lands on the floor, followed by mine. Her hands fumbling with my belt buckle give us enough pause for me to register where we are. The laughs of the men from downstairs. The creaks of the stairs, probably Ma Casey going to her bedroom. This house is not built for what I want my first night back with this girl, this woman, to be.

I flee to the other side of the room—still not far enough—and stuff my hands in my pockets to not reach for her. Doing that here doesn't feel right anymore. I have zero interest in a one-night stand, hushed up so her family doesn't know.

"I want to hear you scream my name," I tell her.

Her eyes twinkle. She runs into my chest and hugs me the same way her Ma does. With abandon and love. "Don't leave. We can just . . . talk."

"Talk?" I say into her blue hair. She smells so good. Part dish soap, part I'm not sure, but it's intoxicating. "Do you have enough self-restraint for both of us?"

"No. But I don't have something better than a sword to put between us."

"Tristan and Isolde. Nice."

Dark but not stormy, or rather stormy-for-a-good-reason eyes regard me. "You read?"

"I played Tristan once. Familiar with the sword scene." I twirl a strand of her indigo hair around my finger. "What's better than a sword?"

"I have zero condoms. You?"

Shit. She's right. I didn't plan on sleeping with anyone on this trip. "No."

"I am not on the pill, and I have a bad history with IUDs. So, it's condoms or pass for me. The whole baby idea should send enough fear into you."

If she only knew. "There are other ways to have sex."

"Shh. We should probably not say those words out loud in this house. I swear the walls have ears, and Mum might decide to come say goodnight to me, which she hasn't done the whole week I've been back."

"Can't you lock the door?"

Siobhan gives me a face like I've asked if the sun rises in the west. "This door has never, ever had a lock. What self-respecting Catholic family would allow their teenage daughter to have a lock on her door?"

The door of my room in my parents' house in Malibu has had a lock since I was sixteen. Dad walked in on me hooking up with my first girlfriend. The next day I had a lock on the door, a box of condoms on the nightstand, and a note saying to use them both.

"The threat of your mother walking in on us is a good enough deterrent."

"Wanna test that theory?" Siobhan tugs me to her twin bed, and I jam myself between the wall and her warm body. Sitting with a full erection in jeans is uncomfortable. Taking the jeans off is not an option. I adjust my position and catch her eyes on my crotch.

"Don't pay attention to what's going on below the belt. Haven't had any action since our night together, and not for a year before then."

"I take that"—she points to my jeans—"as a compliment."

"As you should. Just a dangerous one."

"And I love danger." The smile that spreads across her face doesn't help my below-the-belt situation. She licks her lips, and I have to suppress a groan.

"Remember the sword."

"Fecking sword." Siobhan takes a decorative pillow with her ma's embroidery, similar to one I got last year as a Christmas present, and tosses it to me along with my shirt. "This will have to do. Ma's words will guard us when we are weak."

I laugh when I read the pillow:

> May green be the grass you walk on,
> May blue be the skies above you,
> May pure be the joys that surround you,
> May true be the hearts that love you.

The pillow works. Siobhan putting her shirt back on also helps. Mostly. We talk.

"I have almost one hundred designs in my portfolio," she says into the cotton of my shirt, curled by my side in her bed. My arm went numb twenty minutes ago, listening to her talk about her passion, but I'd let my entire body go numb to keep this feeling.

"I passed the blood pathogen certification last month and am set to start my apprenticeship with Caleb in January. He's the one who did three of my last tattoos based on my designs." She lifts her shirt and shows me the blue flowers on her ribcage, the lotus on her shoulder that I don't remember seeing during our night together, and a Celtic knot behind her left ear. Are there any changes to the dreamcatcher design on her thigh I enjoyed last time? Nope, not thinking about that.

"I won't earn any money for a while, so I'll work the mornings at the Diamond Club, and the afternoons and evenings will be at the shop. No days off, but the fact that Caleb took me on is a miracle." Without pausing for a breath, she carries on. "I'm only the second apprentice he's had in his over twenty-year career. I can't disappoint him. You have to see more of his work." She pulls out her phone, and we browse through pictures of colorful and intricate body art for another hour.

Owen's signature knock I know from the dorms at Trinity interrupts our conversation. "Can I come in or should I just talk through the door?" Owen whispers through the gap between the door and the casing. If we can hear him this well, what would anyone standing in his place in the hallway hear? Not having sex in this room was the smartest idea I've had in a while.

"Come in," Siobhan answers before I react.

Owen opens the door a crack and steps through in time for Siobhan to grab the pillow from my lap and throw it at her brother's face.

"Shiv, for God's sake. I have to get married tomorrow. You can't both go at my face before the big night."

"You're right. I should've gone with your balls so Teresa could have a calm restful night, instead of waiting on your hairy arse."

"So mature." Owen switches his attention from his sister to me. "Don't know what you see in this one."

I open my mouth to tell him it's none of his business.

"But it's none of my business. Adults. I heard you both earlier. Loud and clear." He raises his hands. "Don't kill me now, but I need my best man awake and helpful on my wedding day tomorrow, so let's head to the bunk, mate."

"You go." Siobhan touches her lips to mine. Neither of us moves. "Go," she says against my mouth.

"Going," I say without adding space between us.

"I can't look at you two. This is embarrassing. All those Hollywood romance roles made you soft, mate." Owen takes my hand and drags me off the bed.

From Cparks@uknews.uk

To: JacksonHarper@pulicisagency.com

Re: Asher Menken - Open Immediately - URGENT

Nine

Asher

Judging by the breakfast left for the men in the oven, Ma Casey must have been up at the crack of dawn this morning. There is no time for explanations or lengthy conversations. I've arranged to move everyone into the hotel and we have to get the men, including Brendan, into their tuxedos. Brendan's aversion to pants is making it difficult. Besides a brief sighting of blue hair and a flash of green dresses, we don't see the women the entire morning.

Everything is a blur. Siobhan is stunning as fourth bridesmaid. This is my first full Catholic mass and it takes forever. The photo session is interrupted by rain. Twice. One of the limousines stuck in mud. But I can't help smiling.

My best friend is married. His bride looks beautiful. Every Casey in the county made the trip, it seems, and they're beaming. And my Little Star—yes, *my*—has been whispering in my ear all day every naughty thing she's going to do to me tonight in my hotel room. The last one involved my tie and me not being able to move until she's done with me. I might need to wear ties more often. How have I never been tied to a bed before? The wrought iron headboard at the hotel will be a perfect place to start.

Finally, we sit down. Owen and Teresa occupy a separate table with gold *Mr. and Mrs.* letters in cursive writing on display, and more of the green and gold décor dominates the reception room. I thought a Christmas wedding would be tacky, but the evergreen boughs, leafy green holly, and white poinsettias give the reception an air of elegance. Three long tables accommodate the rest of the wedding guests, who are moving aside tiny herbal bouquets and staring at the gold letters on the emerald à la carte menu with more words in French than English.

Teresa's hand is in all of this, and I understand why Ma Casey wasn't on board with her daughter-in-law's decorating choices. When the head of the family saw the herbal crown on top of the moss green and gold fondant-covered tiers as the only decoration for the wedding cake, I had to hug her in sympathy.

"What's 'Blanquette de Veau?'" Catriona asks Quinn to my right.

"She could've added the English translation," I hear Ma Casey say from across the table.

"It's on the beige page insert, see?" Siobhan picks up the single sheet covered in English.

No one complains about the French names once the food arrives, and everyone at the table has at least three rounds of drinks. I take my phone out of my breast pocket to snap a pic of the menu as a reminder for my next event. I ignore the string of notifications on the home screen. The darned thing's been buzzing like a banshee, but I refuse to pay attention. I should've left it in the room, but I want lots of photos from tonight. I never want to forget this day.

The kids dive into their crêpes and Siobhan licks the spoon after she's done with her soufflé. I finish my delectable Tartiflette. I can't pass up on a potato dish no matter the country of its origin. The bacon and gooey cheese warm me from inside out in two bites. This is what happiness feels like. A guy could get used to it.

I marvel at the smiles on every face around the table: the friends, aunts, uncles, cousins I've met or never seen before. Ma's chattering with a gaggle of women, pointing at me every now and again. I've had to sign a few napkins, but mostly everyone treats me like one of the family. Feels good to let my guard down and just be.

The band starts the music, and we turn to watch my best friend and his new wife take to the floor for the first dance. Siobhan's hand finds mine, and I bring my lips close to her ear. "You want to be next?" I ask.

"On the dance floor?" Excitement brightens her eyes, and I don't correct her. My mind tricks me into thinking we could be Mr. and Mrs., the central attraction at the next Casey wedding. No rush. I've all the time in the world to take this slow, do things right. First dating, then proposal, then marriage, then kids. Kids. A sliver of the pain of Leyla's decision threatens to mar the moment. Siobhan squeezes my hand, and the ache disappears.

I stand up and race her to the gathering crowd on the raised hardwood dais. We join the high-octane tune everyone dances to, and I make a fool of myself, jumping around her and treasuring her pink cheeks, the blue hair flying around her face, and an occasional peek-a-boo of her Celtic knot tattoo. Owen slams into me, and I ram him right back. "Eejit," we both yell through laughter.

The music shifts and the backbeat melts into a symphony of sweet low notes. The slow dance gives us a chance to catch our breath. I wrap my arms around Siobhan's waist, pull her close, and stare into her dark-green-today irises. The floor-length, long-sleeved emerald dress covers her neck to foot. The style shows none of the body art she's created.

"I'm wondering"—I can't help teasing her—"are you still a fan of matching things?" I grab a strand of her indigo-dyed hair hoping she gets the reference to our run-in in the bathroom months ago.

"Only if I decide to wear underwear."

She one-ups me again. I'm falling for this woman. "I love . . . this color," I say, instead of "you."

"Don't get used to it. I change my hair color on a dime. Might be purple tomorrow."

"I love the way you are true to yourself." I reach out and slide my finger over the silky material covering up too much. "I want the world to see all of you. As I see you. Beautiful, bold, brilliant."

"Is that a line from one of your movies?"

"No."

"Well, it's a good one." Her arms tense. "You know, being with me won't be easy. People will judge."

Is this what she's worried about? This I can fix. "Let 'em. I only care about you. What you think. Want. Need."

She doesn't relax. Her eyes study the floor. "I'm hard to live with."

"I like a challenge." My finger lifts her chin, asking her to look at me. She acquiesces. "You're worth any risk."

My words get my now favorite smile.

"Won't be easy with me either." I didn't want to have this conversation so soon, hoped the bubble of bliss would last longer, but she needs to understand what she's getting herself into once we leave this place. I've dealt with the press all my life. Found ways to live with fame and its trappings. "There'll always be the press, the chains of being a star." She's gazing at me so intently, my heart constricts. "But I promise, I'll always be on your side, standing right there with you. If you'll let me."

For a moment, I fear she'll take my words to heart and run, but I should never underestimate my Little Star. She touches her nose to mine. "You're in for one hell of a ride, fella."

"I'm in for the long haul." And I mean it. Not for today or next week or next year. This is the real deal, true and honest.

"I need to stick my tongue down your throat right now," she breathes into my ear.

I can't say no to her. Don't want to.

The dance floor fills again as the music transforms into an uproar of Celtic rhythms. We slip away through the side door.

The evening air pricks at my heated cheeks. I don't think there's enough light for me to see anything, but I don't care.

I draw Siobhan to my chest and hope she can feel through the thin fabric of my pants and her dress how ready I am for us to be alone in a place that has a normal-sized bed, where we can spend more than mere stolen moments together. Her leg goes around my waist and I slide my hand under the silk of the dress, up her ankle, knee, thigh. I find her round butt cheek and press her closer, while our lips and tongues create a dance of their own.

A flash of light blinds me, then another.

"Asher, Asher, over here!"

Fuck. How did they find me? I step in front of Siobhan to shield her from the flashing cameras.

I know the press is part of the price of fame, but Kenmare is my sanctuary. Did someone tail us from the airport? Is this what the incessant texts from Jackson are about? Was he trying to give me a heads up? I told him about Siobhan after our night together months ago, had to, in case the paparazzi tracked the girl from the video down. He promised to protect her, and to warn me. He knew I was going off the grid for Owen's wedding.

I'm used to the tabloids' harsh words, but I couldn't stand what they said about her in the papers after the Starlight event. Owen's words in the attic haunt me. He's right; these vultures will prey on her because she's different. Oh, how I love how she's different.

My damn phone vibrates again. I need to call Jackson, but first I need to get Siobhan away from the cameras.

"Turn around," I tell Siobhan. "Go back inside."

A man shouts, "Is the baby yours?"

I freeze, unable to move. I peer at Siobhan. I can't help my eyes going to her stomach, my mind doing the mental math.

Is there something she's not telling me? Would she be showing yet? How amazing would that be?

Siobhan catches my eyes on her. "It's not me, you dose."

I shake my head. Of course. Too much, too soon. I grab the back of my neck, open my mouth to apologize, to at least say something, when another reporter shouts at us.

"Are you and Leyla getting back together?"

Why do they always ask this? What in the world makes them think that is ever going to . . . Shit. Cold dread fills my stomach. This isn't happening. She swore she didn't want kids. It was why we broke up. Why I had to leave.

"What? What's wrong?" Siobhan's hand is on my arm, and her irises have fireworks in them from the scattered camera flashes behind me.

Wasn't I good enough?

"Asher. How does it feel to be a daddy?"

But I'm not. It can't physically be possible. Everything is blurring. I can't see straight. I wanted a baby so bad I could taste it. Saw little Leylas running around our house, playdates with our friends, a clan of my own.

There's a tug on my sleeve, and I'm propelled forward. The clicking of the cameras fade, and dark shrouds me again, no more flashing lights.

The baby's not mine. It should have been.

I can't look at my Little Star. This isn't fair. "I gotta go."

★ ★ ★

Trending today on Twitter.

#AshLa

Are Asher and Leyla back together?

#babybump

Mum's the word on Leyla's baby daddy

#Ashersbaby

Rumors swirl Asher Menken is the father of Leyla's baby

Ten

Siobhan

Well, this hit the shitter fast. Can't be a proper Casey wedding without a good whack of drama.

The expression on Ash's face when the reporter asks if he's the father was . . . odd. Then poof, he goes and vanishes.

I try to follow him when Owen appears. "Get back into the hall. Teresa is about to throw the bouquet." He pulls me the wrong direction, back to the reception, away from Ash. Being with Ash is what I want, but fulfilling my bridesmaid duties at my brother's wedding is what's expected of me. I go with what's expected. Me, Teresa's two unmarried cousins, and toddler Kelley fidget on the dance floor for everyone to stare at.

"One, two, three, catch!" The damned flowers make a graceful arc, appearing to lean to the cousin with a long black braid, but she sidesteps at the last moment. The cursed thing falls at my feet. No way was I putting my hands on them, dutiful sister or not. If I touch the bunch, Mum and the rest of the clan will start planning my wedding, because why would anyone *not* believe a stupid superstition? They might not have seen me for seven years, but they must know marriage and I are not things that go together. Kelley picks up the bouquet and tries to give the mess to me. Bless her.

"Keep it, baby. Finders keepers."

Her angelic face shines with happiness, and she hugs the disheveled flowers to her chest.

A whiff of alcohol and wet hands on my arms bring me face-to-face with the inebriated father of the bride. "Doll, you're so pretty, but"—he burps, and I get a secondhand taste of the whiskey he's been drinking—"why ruin yourself with the weird hair?"

And this is why I haven't been home for seven years. It's not all about Mum. Some of it, a lot of it, was about this town, its attitude, its expectations, its assumption that their way was the only right way to live. Yes, I'm only a server at the Diamond Club, but not once has Mrs. Marino, the owner, or any of the staff disparaged me for the color of my hair.

His fingers dig into me as he slides sideways, and a ripping sound crackles in my ears. I steer him to the nearest seat and get him situated. A quick inspection of my dress shows both sleeves have split at the shoulder seams. A tinge of black ink peaks out on my left shoulder.

"Mr. MacCarrick"—Catriona steadies the man on the other side—"your daughter's the most beautiful bride I've ever seen." She pours a glass of water from the pitcher on the table and puts it in front of the slumping man, who's unlikely to remember this moment tomorrow.

"Do you have him? I need to run up to my room for a sweater." I point at the rips on my dress.

"He's no worse than Brendan. At least this one has his pants on. You go on."

Two kids in four years, and I don't think Quin and Catriona plan to stop any time soon. Baby number three is due this summer. Mum must be happy at least one of her clan is providing her with grandchildren. Instead of taking the elevator to my room, I take the stairs straight for Ash's. I knock on the door, but there's no answer. This hotel is the best in town, but it's not that big. I hightail my arse to the business center, but the small space is dark and empty.

The open bar is still bustling as I head back to the reception. I scan the room, hoping Ash is back.

"Not like Asher to miss the cake cutting." Owen plants a kiss on my head. "Thanks for holding the fort, but we're going." He wraps his newly-minted wife in a bear hug. "We'll test what the best room in this place can hold up to." Teresa smacks him playfully and they bolt toward the exit, looking like marriage is the best thing in the world.

I dip into the ladies' room, close the door on the last stall, and reread the flirty texts Ash and I've been sending each other throughout the day. Followed by the latest fifteen variations on "Where are you?"

I text Ash again.

Owen and Teresa have gone to bed.

No little dots. My call goes straight to voicemail.

I've no idea where he might be. I'm trying to keep calm, but this is not looking good. Should I check the two pubs down the street? No, that's a place I'd expect Da to end up, not Ash.

Or is it? I think I know the real Ash, but I may be wrong. He could've gone back to LA. How hard is it to get a private jet on a moment's notice? The Killarney airport is a half-hour away from here; he could fly to Dublin and then straight on from there.

Back to the reception hall it is. If Ash returns, that might be the most central place for us to meet again. Next time we are at an event, we need a dedicated "if we get separated" spot. If Disneyland taught me anything beyond making Belgian waffles, it's that tired and upset people are not the best at keeping their shit together. I'll never forget consoling a little girl who lost track of her mother. Her tears tore at my heart.

"Shiv?" Quinn touches my naked shoulder. Feck, I forgot to get the sweater. I tuck the green silk into my bra strap in a makeshift attempt to cover my skin. "We're going up to our room," he whispers, which is ridiculous, because although the band is gone, there are a dozen mostly drunk or at least very loud guests singing songs and trying to dance. Servers weave around them attempting to pick up beer glasses and uneaten slices of cake while waving off invitations to join the caroling crowd. Brendan sighs on Quinn's shoulder, and the whispering makes sense.

It's after midnight, and I'm surprised Caitriona let Brendan stay with Quinn instead of taking him up with her two hours ago when Kelley started fussing. "You good to help Mum?" His eyes dart to the table where Mum is piling plates one on top of the other while a redheaded server gapes at her. Although they're paid to do clean up and need no such help, my mum doesn't know how to rest. Even after her sixtieth birthday, when Owen suggested they hire extra help to make the cheese with the idea she might retire, Mum laughed in his face. She'll be working as long as she has breath in her, maybe longer.

Bet Ash could get her to slow down.

Where is he? Better not be on his way to Barcelona. Yeah, I googled where Leyla is. Not proud of my paranoia. Last night Ash told me they'd really been broken up for over a year. But what do I truly know? The reporters seemed sure the baby is his.

Don't let the baby be his.

Quinn walks me over to Mum as a trio of baritones break into "The Wild Rover." She takes one glance at my half-torn sleeve, my messy hair and, I'm sure, smeared makeup, and makes the face I've seen a million times growing up—the one of disappointment in her only daughter.

"Were you in a fight?" She tucks one, then the other sleeve into my bra strap.

"Damn it," says Quinn. "Brendan's done a runner. Anyone see him?"

I swivel and spot Brendan's curly head. "Over there." I point, and Mum's efforts come undone. She tries to tuck the material back.

Quinn trots to the middle of the dance floor where Brendan, who seemed sound asleep on his shoulder minutes ago, is jumping up and down in front of the singing guests.

There's a loud crash as the redheaded server drops a pile of plates on the floor. Da is looking at the young kid like he's daft and sways back and forth to his own tune. Jacob and Daniel appear on either side of our father, grab an arm each, and stop the swaying. "Time for beddy-byes, Da."

The singers don't miss a beat. They've moved on to lamenting about greener pastures.

I go to give Da a hug goodnight, and the silk of the dress comes loose again. "Siobhan, stop moving," orders Mum.

This is enough. I'm done. I tug at the material, ripping the satin further. "Never liked this bloody dress anyhow." I catch Mum's eye. "Sorry," I mouth. She shakes her head. The dresses were Teresa's only concession to Mum, who insisted the bridesmaids be covered head-to-toe.

I've almost got the one sleeve off. Out of nowhere, hands appear, pulling on the other side of the shredded material. I meet my favorite pair of eyes. Irises the color of whiskey.

Ash. He's still here.

With a screeching sound, the last of the dratted sleeve comes free, swiftly followed by the other, green material hanging limp in my and Ash's hands. The lotus Caleb finished weeks before my flight here and my lucky bluebird are on full display for the whole wedding party to see.

"Daddy." Brendan's voice is next to me. "Can I have a birdie on my arm like Auntie Shiv?"

"Oh, did Siobhan get a new dress? That's pretty"—my father hiccups—"dear." He fails to whisper to Jacob, "Don't get these LA fashions." The servers at the back of the room hear him.

"Jesus, Mary, and Joseph," Mum cries, and I glance at her. She's gone pale and looks like she might faint. I grab a chair and push her into it. For a moment even the rambunctious singing stops. Everyone in the reception hall stands staring at me. "Oy, all of yous, go close up before someone ends up at the hospital."

Quinn looks at Ash, who seems to be the only sober person in the room. "You go," Ash tells him. "I'll handle this."

Ash claps his hands to get everyone's attention. "Okay, show's over, folks. Time to wrap this up." He runs his hand along my exposed arm and gives me a look. The look. Like he knows what he's doing. And he does. "Ah, Mrs. O'Leary, let me help you with your coat." He begins to coax the stragglers out one by one.

I take a seat on the floor by Mum's chair. Her eyes roam across my shoulders, my arms, and I can see her catalogue my every tattoo, every color and shape. "Oh, my Baby Girl." She takes my wrist.

"I have more, you know." I let her run her fingers over the star. "And I'll get more."

"What have I done to make you hate yourself so much?" Mum's hand lands on my neck, and she pulls my head onto her lap. "You're such a pretty girl. I thought the doodling and the makeup was just a phase. You were supposed to go to Trinity College, get a good job, have a happy life. But happy daughters don't run away from home, don't mar their beautiful skin, make themselves"—she strokes my blue locks—"unrecognizable. Hide behind garish colors and flighty fashions."

"Mum, I'm not hiding. Not anymore. I'm showing the world who I am. Making art. My art." I push my face against where her hand strokes my cheek. "You don't have to worry about me."

"Not worry? You'll see how you feel when your daughter moves to the other side of the world from you. You were my surprise baby. I thought we were close. What went wrong between us?"

"I wanted to spread my wings, and you wanted me to be safe. Our visions of my future were opposite."

"You could've told me. I would've listened. Didn't need to leave without telling anyone. LA"—she shakes her head, silver hair shimmering in the overhead lights—"that vulgar place full of liars and scam artists. They don't even cook their fish properly there. The city has no heart."

"But it's my home, Mum. I chose LA. I've built a life there."

"Life." She huffs. "You're a bartender."

"I won't be one forever. I have a plan. I'm hoping to become a tattoo artist in a couple of years. Soon I'll have a stable job and be doing something I love. Following my dreams"—I meet her gaze—"like you did."

"Why can't you do that here? At home? Where your family lives?"

"Home is where your heart longs to be. The Shiv who lived here was a different person. The real me, the Siobhan you refuse to acknowledge, her home is in LA, where she wears short sleeves showing off her body art, dyes her hair every shade of the rainbow, and doesn't have to fit any mold, because different is what fits."

"I know." Her eyes fall to her lap. "I should've let you do your art. I'm sorry. It didn't seem practical. What job does one have as an artist? Starving artist is an expression for a reason. But I see your passion now."

"I was wrong, too, Mum." I try to get her to face me. "I shouldn't have left the way I did. And I shouldn't have stayed away so long. I didn't realize how much I missed being here. How much I missed you. I'll come home more often. I promise."

She sniffs. "You promise? I'm not getting any younger here. Da turns seventy next year. We might not be alive if you don't come back for another seven years." Ah, there it is. The guilt trip.

"You could come visit me. You don't even need visas."

"What is there for us in LA? Can you see me on a beach or shopping in an expensive store or eating sushi?"

"Me. I'm there." I place our entwined hands over my heart. "You can just visit me, not LA. And California is a beautiful place. We can go to other farms, to forests, to the mountains, to the desert. Have you ever seen the desert?"

"Don't be daft. What would I do with a desert?"

And the no-nonsense Mum's back. I catch Ash's eye. Everyone is gone except us. His raised eyebrows ask if it's safe to approach. I nod.

He kneels down beside Mum. "Hey Ma, how're we doing?"

"Asher, my handsome boy. Will you look after my girl out in LA? Find a nice boy to marry her?"

"Mum!" I pick myself up off the floor and avoid Ash's eyes. Now is not the time to announce we are . . . well, whatever

Ash and I are. I'm not even sure if we are an 'us.' Maybe the baby is his. Maybe he came back to say goodbye. I take a chance. "Actually, I already found one, and he likes me for who I am."

"Oh?" Mum's misty eyes from a moment ago are gone, replaced by a sharp piercing stare. "Will I approve of him?"

"I know you're gonna like him." I give her a hug. "But I think right now we need to get to bed. There's plenty to do in the morning. Teresa will need lots of help."

That perks Mum up. Ash and I get Mum into her room, where Da is already snoring at top volume. Minutes later, we're in Ash's suite, alone at last. He didn't even ask if I'd join him, just offered me his arm and led me to his room. That has to be good, right?

Ash plops down beside me on the little sofa at the end of the bed. I find his fingers and pull his hand over to me.

"Thanks for the support back there." I nod at my exposed arms.

"Happy to help. About time your family understood how amazing you are." He raises my hand to his lips. "Sorry I disappeared. Had to call my agent and get the truth out about the baby not being mine."

"Smart," is all I can come up with. Inside, I squeal. The baby is not his. He's free. Free to be mine.

"You know," he gives me that movie star smile of his, "the paparazzi have this place surrounded. We might have to hole up in this room for a few days."

"A few days?" I try not to smile, but it's pretty hard.

"Yup. At least."

I clutch his tie and pull him close. "Mister, I'm gonna keep you tied up for weeks."

Ash leans in even closer and nips my ear. "I can't wait."

Want the exclusive FREE Epilogue of Star Struck?

Go to the next page to sign up for our newsletter, and it's yours.

If you liked this book, please consider giving it a review, so others can enjoy it as well.

Epilogue

The bottom bunk in Owen's room is nowhere near as wide as the queen we made good use of at the hotel after Owen and Teresa's wedding, but at least double the width of the bed in my room across the hall. I throw a last glance at Ash's sleeping form in the pre-dawn shadows as I slip out of his embrace.

"Already?" Ash mumbles without opening his eyes. His fingers twitch across the sheets and brush my wrist. The hairs on my arm rise at his touch. Again.

After all the touching that went on in that hotel room and him holding me the entire night, this simple brush of skin against skin shouldn't send electricity right through me. But it does. Every time he touches me, I light up like a Christmas tree.

For more, sign up for our newsletter. Scan the QR Code below to get there or email us at willadrewauthor@gmail.com and we'll get you on the list.

Siobhan and Asher will be back in Star Light in 2023.

Add Star Light to your Goodreads Reading List today.

Acknowledgements

First and foremost, thank you for reading this book.

Fellow writer Estelle Pettersen challenged us to write a short story for her "The Busy Romantic's Five-Minute Read" on Wattpad. We already had a universe created for our first collaboration, Kisses, Lies, & Us. Siobhan was a side character who we laughed with, shouted at, and couldn't get out of our heads.

A year into the pandemic Gala suffered from major wanderlust. She scrolled through photo after photo of her latest trip to Ireland. Unable to fly there, she persuaded DL to use the magic of their words to create a quaint Irish town they could both escape into.

Exercising with a beautiful and courageous instructor with bright pink hair and intricate tattoos kept Gala sane and served as inspiration for our heroine. Siobhan's hair might be teal, but she has the same intrepid spirit.

DL is usually glued to the screen during the Oscars from the first moment the stars step onto the red carpet until they give out the Best Movie award eight hours later. Low and behold in one of her famous shower-induced inspirations, Asher stepped off the red carpet.

The dreamy rom-com star told DL his acting days were over. It was time to take control of his life, and making movies was his new calling. Go figure. (If you liked Chapter 3, that was the product of another hot shower.)

Because we share a love of Ireland, we wanted the language to be authentic. Enter Sinead. She kindly answered our barrage of questions including the difference potatoes and pratties, luv and leahbh, and other Irishisms.

We both have many writer friends to thank. The LOL35 ladies: our worldwide writing and life help line that got us over some of our worst lows and were there to celebrate the highs–you rock! The Sweet and Sassy Writers group: our beta readers and cheerleaders who encouraged us to publish our first book.

The thank you list of people from Wattpad would take up too many pages, but your comments, ideas, and support helped. You know who you are, and we love reading your stories.

Without the amazing talent of our editors, everything would be grey (not gray), there would be characters with three hands, and some guests under the table. And how can we forget about swapping comments on the difference between bop and jiggle? Thank you, Julie Sherwood, Kay Springsteen, and Victoria Flickinger.

If you like the drawing of Asher and Siobhan on our cover (and we sure do), María Peña is the girl to contact.

Books and Moods took María's artwork and created our beautiful cover. Thanks, girls.

Of course, this story, like all our writing adventures, would not be possible without the support of our families.

Gala: I would like to thank: my husband, who protected my writing time, and endured hours of conversations about my stories; my kids, for keeping my curiosity alive; my parents and in-laws who didn't balk when I told them I started writing romance.

Thank you, Milana, for letting me borrow your looks and spirit for Siobhan. Thank you, Flynn, Carrie, and Natalia for encouraging me to stick with the whole writing things. Thank you Mirjam and Caitlin for our Saucy Laundry conversation that always make my day brighter. Thank you, PH for helping me make the right decisions along the writing path. Thank you, Jim, for your sage advice. And thank you to my book club for giving me the first seed of "Maybe I can write too?" idea. You all contributed an ingredient that got me to this first book.

Thank you to my laughing-until-we're-both-crying, patient co-writer. I have a very short list of people who changed the course of my life, and she is on it. At the time we are writing these acknowledgments we haven't even met in person. Can you believe it? And we wrote so many stories together. The mindmeld we plunge into during writing and editing is such a high, it feels like it should be illegal. She knows more about me than I care to admit. I treasure her positivity, her belief that our dreams are coming true, her creativity, and relentless drive to bring joy to others one romance at a time.

DL: Thank you feels too small a word to express my awe that Gala wanted to hop on this mad journey into the world of writing with me. I have no idea why she chose me to be her writing partner (there seemed way more qualified candidates), but I thank my lucky stars she did. I've laughed so hard, cried a little, and created magical spells in the form of stories with you. Let's never stop doing this. A huge shout out to Gala's husband and children for letting me spend endless hours (they would say too many) with her.

To my fabulous friends who insist they are not sick of me droning on and on about my writing, thanks for sticking with me.

To my mother, father, and brother, I'm sorry I missed all those dinners and phone calls. But look — I wrote a book!

Willa Drew is not one, but two writers of fun, flirty fiction full of feels.

Lovers of emotional scenes (don't tell anyone: someone always cries as we write them), dramatic scenarios (don't blame us, the characters insisted), and the best the world has to offer like eclairs and butter tarts (don't ask us to share, but we'll point you to the recipes).

Our young adult and new adult romances have every flavor. Angst? Check. Secrets? Of course. Risk taking? You bet. Expect slow burns, heart flutters, soul mates, first loves, and swoon-worthy kisses.

Hang out with us over on all the socials @willadrewauthor or get sign up for our newsletter and get updates sent right to you.

SNEAK PEEK

WE BLEND

"WE" SERIES BOOK #1

ONE

FAME FOLLOWS ME EVERYWHERE.

Not today. This morning I'm invisible. Everything is going according to plan and twelve hours crammed upright in an airplane seat were a small price to pay for my freedom. London commuters rush by on their way to work as I stroll back to my hotel sipping my average cup of Joe. No bodyguard in sight.

A smattering of paparazzi in front of the marble staircase sends my heart beating faster. No. They can't know I'm here. Can they? I tug the brim of my baseball cap. I look nothing like myself. Maybe I should've picked a smaller hotel, but the Four Seasons is where Dad always stays. Lots of celebrities choose it.

I rush past the cameras and try not to groan at how long the doorman takes to open the wrought iron doors. Inside the hotel, it's quiet and calm. Made it.

"Melodie." I hear my name ring across the gleaming two-story lobby.

A shiver shoots up my spine. "Dad?"

I look over to the plush maroon couches arranged in a semi-circle, and sure enough, there's Bill Rockerby. Stepdad to me. Rocker to the world. That's who the press is here for. He's not even hiding his rockstar status, decked out in black leather like he just walked off the stage after one of his concerts. Except he's walking toward me, his mouth pressed into a thin line, the look of disappointment I dread souring the handsome face lots of women, and men, drool over.

"What are you doing here?" I stumble over my words.

"The better question is, what are you doing here?" His voice is low and tense.

"I—" I don't have a comeback. Truth: I'm supposed to be in New York on a shopping spree, chaperoned by my mother-approved cousins, not in this swanky hotel in London.

His hand is on my arm. "Not here." Amber eyes dart left and right and back again. "People are listening." Dad's always paranoid about the press, especially in Europe. He corrals me toward the elevator, presses the call button, and we stand in awkward silence as we wait.

My mind races between two thoughts. Was it Bailey or Zoe who spilled the beans? 'Cause they were supposed to cover for me and not fold less than twenty-four hours into my escape. We have a pact: provide alibis for each other when we need to escape the parental cages, but their end of the bargain is harder to uphold. And I've never left the country by myself before. Zoe asked me five times if I was sure about the ruse.

More important: How do I get out of this?

There's a soft ding, probably a D-flat but the pitch is off a hair, and the gold doors slide open. I jump in first, hit the button for my floor; Dad follows close behind. More silence, like the pause between songs on a playlist. The doors close, and the elevator jumps to life.

"Your mother is sick with worry."

Slash. His words are tiny shavings of metal cutting at me. He knows my weak spot. Making Mom anxious, given what she's going through, is one of the worst things I could do. I squeeze my teeth together and don't reply because I've never learned to lie. My parents' publicist keeps trying to coach me, but the closest I can get is to omit the truth. Ask me a direct question, and I'll blabber, but I can't tell Dad about why I'm here.

"You can't silence your way out of this mess. Is it Dillon? I called him as soon as your mother got the alert on her credit card about the hotel charge." The elevator is playing a Muzak version of Justin's *Holy*, and my ears want to bleed. "He pretended he hadn't heard from you—better at lying than your cousins."

Mom's card. The receptionist said they had to have one in case I have other charges but promised they won't use it as long as I pay cash. Months of saved allowance was just enough for a ticket, three nights at the hotel, food, and paying for my music video. I'm not staying at this chain anymore. All the talk about keeping their clients' confidentiality, and they sell me out to my parents within hours.

"Talk to me." His voice softens a bit, and he angles his body toward me. "I might be forty-two, but I remember what being young and in love was like. I thought you were over him. With him back in England, you stopped pining for the asshole, pardon my French."

Dillon. Right. If I agree I'm here for Dillon, Dad might not dig deeper. My plan might still have a chance. "I thought I loved Dillon." It's true. I did think that. I don't anymore, but I let Dad draw his own conclusions. I keep squeezing my teeth. I can do it. Don't say anything, don't say anything, don't say anything.

"And what was your thought process? Fly across the ocean, profess your love for him, and hope, what? That he'll ditch his new job and come back to the States for you?"

New job? Is that why he left? He didn't offer me an explanation when he sent me his "I'm sorry, I can't do this" text.

I don't trust myself to speak, so I shrug instead.

"It's been six months."

The elevator doors open, and I trudge to my room, push the heavy door, and sink onto the king-size bed, leaving the chair by the desk for Dad to sit in. The calm gray-blue hues of the room cool the emotions circulating between us.

"You know you don't have to lie."

I want to scream "I do. You won't let me do anything otherwise."

"You know we love you."

"I know." This one's no lie. If anything, they love me too much. So much, there's no room for anything else.

"And that we do these things to protect your privacy. To keep you safe from another paparazzi-triggered breakdown. Can you blame your mother for wanting a semblance of normalcy for you?"

"Nope." After what happened to Papa and me, I can never blame her for wanting to keep me safe. But I don't have to like it. The bubble-wrapped life is smothering me. Sometimes I feel like I can't breathe between the rules, the bodyguards, and the ever-narrowing circle of things to do or people to do them with. Probably not a good time to bring up my complaints. Today, I need all suspicion away from the true reason I'm in London. And it isn't Dillon.

"I'll call your mom while you pack, tell her you're safe. The pilot's getting the jet ready for us."

"But . . ." If I don't show up to my meeting with Mr. Astor tomorrow, I'll lose the fifty percent down payment I transferred. "Can I at least go talk to Dillon?" I run my hand through my hair, find the familiar strands that always feel different, out of place, and pull, causing just enough pain to distract me from spilling the truth. The pain merges with the cloud of cutting metal of Dad's words.

"Why do you want to go down that road?" Dad puts his Doc Martin on his knee and shakes his foot. "No. You're not leaving this room until I escort you to the plane. It's nonnegotiable."

"But, Dad—"

"Melodie." He touches my hand, and I stop with the hair.

I focus on my tennis shoes and not on the buzzing shrapnel in my chest.

"Look at me."

I do as he says, because I'm a good girl.

"Leave it be."

Damn. There is no getting out of this. I'll have to message Lenard Astor and figure out a way, another time we can find two days in his schedule. Even if I do lose part of the money, I'll make it up with several months' of my allowance, if I buy nothing at all.

"Oh, and since you insist on being treated like an adult, it's time you took on some adult responsibilities. How about getting a job?"

"This again. I don't even have a high school diploma. How would it look if your stepdaughter asks 'do you want fries with that' for a living?"

"I wouldn't mind as long as you're happy."

He always says stuff like this. Cares almost too much. Unlike Mom who loves me but uses the tough-love parenting style. Nice or not, my music is my priority. "How can I be happy doing that when what I'd make at such a place is pennies compared to my allowance."

"Your mother wants to cut off your allowance as well."

"She can't. I have expenses." The metal ball of doom swings on a chain, and I cling to it, not wanting to wreck my plans.

"Really?" His bushy eyebrow performs that sky high thing it does when he's being sarcastic. "We pay for everything."

"I need clothes."

"You have two walk-in closets."

"I was going to buy a new keyboard."

"What's wrong with the one in the studio?"

"That's yours."

"I have a solution. Why don't you come and work for me at Rocker, Inc. Nadine needs help in the back office. It'll give you some work experience and you can help discover the next *it* artist."

I don't want to discover them, I want to *be* them. But I need the money to start again, and working for my stepfather isn't the worst thing in the world. "What's the starting salary?"

He smiles for the first time. "You make it sound like you're doing me a favor here and not the reverse. I'll pay you the same as I'd pay anyone I'd hire to do the job. And no special treatment. You'll be like any of my other employees."

It's not as if I have a lot of choice here. "Fine."

I grab the suitcase Mom gave me for my eighteenth birthday and fling the lid open. I stuff the ten outfits I brought for my stay into it and hide my sheet music under the top dress. My independence day's gone. Guess it's back to the US for the Fourth of July.

"This is ridiculous." The bright yellow Louis Vuitton with my initials monogrammed in blue, MVR for Melodie Vella Rockerby, mocks my ruined dreams with its bright cheer.

"You running away is what's ridiculous." His phone dings an F-sharp, and he answers.

"Yes. I'm with her. Yes. Safe." I can feel his eyes on my back as I snap my suitcase shut. "I told her the terms. Love you too."

He puts the phone down and gets up. "I have to go make an excuse to the press. They spotted me at Southend when I landed. Wait for me here. Hotel security has someone by your door. Don't even try talking to them."

The lead ball drops from my chest into my stomach at the sight of the security guard when Dad leaves my room. I grab onto the doorframe and take a moment to survey the hallway, looking for possible escape routes.

"Get inside and stay there." Patience is no longer in Dad's voice, and I want to scream. Instead, I slam the door.

The heavy metal doesn't connect but bounces off the fingers on my left hand, still clutching the white casing. I jerk them toward me and watch the indentations on the index and middle finger bloom pink. At the sight, the numbness disappears, replaced by blinding pain. The scream I've wished for erupts from my lungs. I suck air and glare at the places where the edge of the door tore through the skin. It doesn't look that bad. That's when the throbbing begins, and I can barely hear Dad barking orders at the guard to get the hotel doctor.

This is not how I imagined my first jail break would go.

TWO

I haven't been in LA for more than five minutes, and he walks right by me. So close, I can almost smell his designer cologne. A few steps, and I could slap him on the back, assuming I could get past the security detail.

My father. The rockstar.

Bill Rockerby strolls through the airport, his entourage carrying bright yellow luggage like little ducks in a row, while I stand here at baggage claim waiting for mine like a normal person.

Is that his stepdaughter in the back? She sure lucked out when her mother remarried, getting a rockstar as her new father. Some tossers get all the breaks. She doesn't look happy about being home. One hand sports a splint binding her fingers together. Did Daddy's little girl's vacation get ruined? Poor her. Not.

The sunglasses that hold up her red hair surely cost more than my entire wardrobe. Her signature streak falls on the left side of her face. If not for that shock of white, from this close she looks more like a girl next door than the glossy spoiled brat in the pages of the magazines Mum used to bring home from the clinic. Without the makeup and the posh clothes, her beauty shines. Not my type, but plenty of people would love to have someone like her as their arm candy.

Whispers start around me, and phones turn in their direction. Some brave souls take a few steps to get closer, others shout about getting a selfie. Rocker and Melodie keep walking. We're nothing but an annoyance to them. They could've smiled, waved, but no, not rock-n-roll's elite. They press on with sour faces and disappear from view.

"I almost touched him," a bloke in denim overall shorts and flip-flops gushes to the girl next to him. American fashion is not something I'll ever understand.

I unzip the inside pocket of my GOODBOIS messenger bag, the one nice thing I own, and get out the small notebook covered in black faux leather. With a pop, the pencil snaps out of the elastic holder, and I jot down:

Annoyance on the clean face or a perfect smile on
a glossy page

sound of flip-flops on a linoleum floor
Almost. Always almost.

Notebook safely tucked away, I roll up the sleeves of my dark green shirt. Mum's been supplying me with the pocket notebooks ever since I started writing up the ideas that pop into my head on my hands and arms. There's a drawer full of them at home and two more in my pack that, with any luck, is not lost. I shift the beat-up guitar case from my feet and onto my shoulder and walk closer to the conveyor belt.

Time to let Mum know I've arrived. I connect my phone to the free airport Wi-Fi, pull up WhatsApp, and type "I'm here." She'll relay the message to Opa, who doesn't get the whole text-message thing. I can hear my grandfather grumbling, "Why can't you just pick up the phone?" Even though it's midnight in Bremen, I get a barrage of messages back. Mum should be sleeping, she needs it, but I type back some deets.

The LAX Airport Shuttle bus goes to the Transit Center, where I catch the Number 3 Big Blue Bus, which gets me to Westwood for fifty cents. My kind of price. I get off and make sure my backpack doesn't hit anyone when I turn—the top part is higher than my head, and I'm taller than most men around me. A short walk, and I arrive at the UCLA campus. It has people, but it's quiet, unlike the one I just left. Had to bail on the rest of the semester for this, but I'll be back in time for the October session.

There are a few people around, and I catch the eye of two beauties lying on a blanket on the grass. They both smile at me, and I make sure to return the gesture. I may be here for serious business, but that doesn't mean a fella can't have fun in the process.

Part of me can't believe my luck in getting into the program. I applied to the Starlight Future Filmmakers Foundation's annual film competition as a laugh. I never thought I'd get a call for the audition. The committee gave me the option to fly in or do it over Zoom. Yeah, 'cause I have the dough to drop on a trip to LA for a bloody interview. Harder to turn on my charm over the internet, but I made it work, and here I am—an almost-all-expenses-paid trip to the U.S. of A.

Checking in to the dorms is the simplest thing I've done today. Let the free ride begin. After the airfare, the credit card I usually only use for emergencies is almost at its limit. Finding a job will be one of the first things on my list. I stick my key into the door but before I turn it, the pale wood slat opens, and a bloke with a buzz cut smiles at me.

"Welcome, bienvenidos, bienvenue—all the languages I know."

"Willkommen," I say.

"Ah, isn't that what they say in Germany?"

"Yup. Born and bred there, so I can vouch for that."

"More of us internationals." He scratches his head. "What's with the British accent?"

"That's ten years learning English at school in Bremen plus summers with family in Sussex."

"Willkommen then, Mr. German."

"It's Wil Peters actually."

"I'm Mateo. Mateo Gallardo." He opens his arms and steps away, so I can enter. The common room isn't a fancy resort, but the light is good, and we're far away from the stairwell. In the middle there's a pair of brown leather couches separated by a low glass table, dominated by a flat screen TV hanging on the wall. Pushed up against the window is a wooden table with six matching chairs. Home sweet home.

"You're the last to arrive, so the only bed left is in my room." He points to the second door on the left. "Me and the other dudes were about to head out and grab some grub. Wanna join?"

I want to drop my stuff and take a shower, but some food wouldn't be bad either. "Sure. Any idea where I can get a SIM card around campus?"

"I'm your man. I scouted all the things we're going to need in this country."

"Including a grocery store? The website said there's a kitchen I can use on this floor." I've learned over the last year living on campus how much Mum did for me. First time I did laundry, I washed my clothes in one load. I still have the shirt that used to be white and is now a combination of gray and splotches of blue. Cooking is another thing I had to figure out.

"You're ambitious. It's just for three months. One thing my mami never let me do is cooking. I already miss her empanadas."

Mateo shrugs as he follows me into the room we are to share. Why do the people who design dorms lack imagination? They're all the same. Two single beds pushed against opposite walls, one night table, and what I presume is a closet the size of a coffin.

I drop my backpack on the bed and prop my guitar in the small space against the wall.

"You here to make a movie too?" Mateo sits down on his bed.

"Yeah, I'm the sound person."

"Way cool." He taps his chest. "Set designer. I'm on the green team."

"Green?"

"Each team has a color. Don't worry." Why would I worry? "You'll get one at the orientation session tomorrow. We can go together in the morning. Already checked out the building."

Seems my luck is holding. Mateo is doing the heavy lifting.

I hang up a classic white long-sleeve shirt Mum snuck in that raises the number of clothing items I brought to eleven. My side of the room looks spartan compared to Mateo's, who on his twelve-hour drive from Mexico brought twice the stuff I had in my old dorm room at uni. I'm particularly impressed with the precise placement of the array of multicolored pens and pencils he's using to draw something in a large notepad. He catches me eyeing them.

"Tools of the trade. I always sketch by hand first."

Day one in the States rushes by in a blur of dropping more money on my credit card. I thought the giant Coke I drank with my first American burger would keep me up but incessant yawning reminds me I've been awake for twenty-four hours.

When I get back from the shower, the bedroom is empty and quiet but for the laughter filtering from the living room where my new flatmates are gearing up to play a video game. I set my alarm for five a.m. so I can fit in a quick workout before orientation. The gym on campus even has rowing machines, so

I can keep up with my crew in Berlin. They'll be rowing on the river daily. Can't get out of shape.

Exhaustion seeps out of me into the mattress, and I stare at the curtains filtering thin pinpoints of light through the top. I'm here. If Opa's right, I'll figure out a way to meet Rocker. I've come the farthest I've ever been from home to talk to the man. And for Mum, I'd go around the world in a rowing boat to improve her health.

The rockstar can spare the money, go without another car or a house in Fiji. It's not like he had to pay child support for eighteen years. What I need is a fraction of what that would've cost him. I'm not looking for a father. Opa filled those shoes for me, but Rocker should help. Mum's done everything for me, her only son. Even if I am just the product of a one-night stand, I'm the only blood offspring that wanker has in this world, and I'm ready to use that fact.

I'm not going home empty-handed.

THREE

El

The dang splint protecting my injured fingers gets stuck in the sleeve of my turquoise dress shirt, and I have to rethink my outfit. No sleeves. I move the hangers in the silver section around until I spot the vintage Paco Rabanne metal chain halter I kept after the Rock Squad Magazine photoshoot for Dad's kids charity fundraiser. The cold links were my armor against the photographer's words telling me where I should stand and what my face should look like. I hang it back up. That is Melodie Rockerby's outfit, not El Vella's.

What will El wear? My stage name is my nod to Papa. Technically, it's still my name, the Rockerby added when Mom married Bill Rockerby. He sat me down and asked if I was okay with him adopting me, explained he never had any kids of his own, would never replace Papa, but he wanted us to be a family. It's not like I could say no. True to his word, Bill, Dad, has always treated me like his, and I do love him. I know I'm lucky, but Rockerby is too famous, too recognizable. No one outside of the opera world will know the last name Vella, which is perfect. I need them to see me.

I tuck my hair behind my ear. What would I wear if I didn't have to think about the tabloids and eventual comments on social media? Something comfortable, because tonight's gonna be tough enough without having to worry about my clothes; something I can keep my cool in, because I'll be sweating all over; something I can sit down in without worrying about showing my underwear.

My last vacation in Malta with Papa's family, I went shopping at the local market and got the most comfortable moss-green palazzo pants that sorta looked like a long skirt, along with a simple white tank top. My arms glide through the holes and my heartrate slows a bit. Memories of the sun and the simple conversations envelop me, offering support. There's something about clothes that sets my mood, and I've found the right ones for El Vella's first stage appearance.

"Are you ready?" Sven asks from behind the closed door. "We have to leave in five." My friend is less than pleased with me since Dad reassigned him from lead bodyguard duty to my personal babysitter. I lucked out, though. If Dad only knew the messes Sven cleaned up for me. There's no one I'd rather have by my side day and night.

Am I really doing it? Stepping on a stage, however small, and not fainting from the greedy eyes trained on me, ready to judge my every wrong word, false pitch, awkward movement? My hands shake when I open the door and follow Sven down the stairs, panting a little too hard. Not good signs, but I have to ignore them. We sneak past the theater room where Mom and Dad are binge watching some historical drama about a queen.

"And where are you going?" Mom's voice stops me in my tracks. I'll need a better route next time.

"Ice cream with Zoe." I've already texted my cousin to cover if my parents get nosey.

"And Sven?" Mom turns around and sees my human shield looming behind me. "Be home by midnight."

I hurry down the hallway before she changes her mind.

Sven opens the back door of the light blue electric Rolls Royce Dad got for my required bodyguard to chauffeur me around, and I slip in. The door clicks shut, surrounding me in silence. Almost. My ears are ringing. My personal Superman jumps in and starts driving us to downtown LA.

Outside the tinted windows, the sky deepens into a purple haze as day morphs into night. Time for my transformation as well. I pull out my phone and follow the instructions on the YouTube video I've watched a hundred times. I finagle my shoulder-length auburn hair into flat twists and cover them with a wig. The platinum locks are longer than my real hair and feel odd falling over my shoulders and down my back to my waist. A little shine on my lips completes the look.

"You are not allowed to go into the actual bar." Sven repeats the instructions he gave me twice before, ignoring my new look. "All the performers under twenty-one have to stay backstage."

"I know."

"I've checked out the place, and I'll be in the back, the left corner closest to the hallway that leads backstage. It'll take me maybe thirty seconds to get to you if you are recognized."

"Left back corner. I got it."

"And you're not talking to anyone but me and Pauline, the manager. You're there to get that job, not have fun at a bar."

"Aye, aye, captain."

"Not funny, Melodie. You don't have to do this. We can turn around and go home." He stops at the red light and looks over his shoulder at me. "There are other ways to get money. Let me help you for once. I'll get a loan and give you the cash, and you'll pay me back once Mr. and Mrs. Rockerby reinstate your allowance."

"Which, according to Mom, is never."

"They're still angry. Give them time."

"I'm angry too."

Sven does his silent listening routine.

"If I'm doing it, and dammit, I am doing it, I'm doing it on my own. I'm not the useless, spoiled baby they think I am. I might not have a formal education"—I air quote the words—"but I had the world's best tutors. Taking the GED seemed more trouble than it was worth. Not like university has ever been in the picture." I sit up straighter, raise my chin, and meet Sven's eyes in the rearview mirror. "But I know a lot about music, and I can earn my own money, live my own life, and be my own person. I don't need them as much as they think I do."

Even though I booked Mr. Astor's last available session in November, my down payment is gone, and the salary at Rocker, Inc. is a start but it's not going to get me the amount I need to cover the cost. Zoe felt bad about the London debacle and offered to make up the difference. After I refused to accept her money, she pulled some strings and snagged me a spot in tonight's open mic competition. The winner gets paid to perform at the Devil's Martini's coveted Saturday night showcase.

This gig alone won't cover the whole sum, but it'll make a big dent. If my plan is to become a singer, why not start now? I've spent enough hours practicing in my room and Dad's home studio to stand a chance. If I win, I prove to everyone I can earn a living with my music.

We enter through a side door of the Devil's Martini, and a preppy young woman in glasses, who looks more like a librarian than someone who'd work at a bar, shoves a clipboard my way.

"Write your name here. You're number five." She hands me a sticker with the number hand-written in red marker. "Are you performing too? Or just the boyfriend?" Her eyes survey Sven's solid body from head to foot, and I swear the top of her cheeks pink up.

"Friend. Audience." Sven gives his standard just-the-facts reply.

"Oh, straight through there, then." Her cheeks are definitely pink when she shows my fair-haired "friend" the way. "And you go left." She switches to me. "You get one song. Hang around till the end, Pauline'll talk to you about the gig if you win. And don't try to butter me up, I'm not one of the judges. Break a leg."

The door slams behind me. She glances at Sven one more time and aims her smile at the next person. We head past her, and I take the door to the left that says, "STAGE. STAFF ONLY," and Sven gives me a thumbs up as he heads up the long hallway and into the bar. I wipe my sweaty palms on the sleek silk crepe of my pants.

The stage is my friend. The stage is my friend.

I'll get on it even if I have to ask someone to push me out. Recording a video for my Project Yellow EP won't happen if I can't perform in front of a crowd. Doubt this dinky bar will even have more than twenty people here, but as long as it's more than zero, it won't be easy.

I knew this day was coming. I just didn't expect it to be this soon. I thought I'd have time. Shoot the video, send it to some producers, make a whole album before I had to perform in front of real live people.

Twenty minutes later, the open mic competition begins, and Jeremiah is not here. My feverish texts go unanswered, and although they have an extra keyboard and a couple of guitars I could use, my broken fingers will take at least five more weeks before I can start using them again. This is what Jeremiah is for: study the music for my songs, bring a guitar, and accompany me. Now what do I do?

I walk up the hallway to the bar area, peek from the door into the room, and scan the place. Jeremiah is steps away, beer in hand, sitting at a dark wooden bar talking with some guy. That jerk. He shouldn't be drinking before we perform. He should be backstage rehearsing, or at least have the decency to answer his phone. I'm not letting him screw this up for me. Google informed me both Dasher and Carlee Waters had their break after winning the open mic competition here. Maybe El Vella can be next.

"Jeremiah," I shout across the room. "Jeremiah, over here."

Jeremiah looks up and meets my eye. Shit, shit, shit. He can barely focus on me. How much has this dufus had to drink? I look at my phone. Our slot is in ten minutes. How can I sober him up? I look for Sven, but he's far off, the librarian's hand on his impressive bicep and his attention on her blazing cheeks and not the bar I'm not even supposed to be in. I don't need him to show up, scare Jeremiah, and end this night before I even get a chance. One eye on Sven, I slink over the black floor to Jeremiah's barstool.

"Jeremiah?" The way his body sways when he moves his head kills any hope of him being my hands today.

"Ellllllll." The happy drunk sings my name. I could kill him. He's no use to me in this state. I side-eye his companion who's drinking . . . water? Odd.

"Meet my new friend. He'sss from Germany. How cooool is that?"

I don't have time to meet people. I need Jeremiah to sober up. I don't have a choice.

"Hey, I'm Wil." I turn to him because my parents taught me manners. His one-sided grin is certain to score, but it's not going to work on me. I'm here on a mission, and it's not a random hook-up with a hot stranger. This is the one time I wish Sven were by my side, so I could get him to remove this playboy. I flick my gaze to Sven to reassure myself he's there and if I scream his name, he'll run over and rescue me.

"Hey. Um, can I talk to Jeremiah? In private."

Light brown, almost golden eyes examine my outfit, the ends of my hair sweeping my hip bones, the exposed skin at my neck, and finishes the round with my face. If I weren't already hot from nerves, that stare would've gotten me there. He's cute, jet-black hair flopping all over the place in that boy-band-wannabe way. He reminds me of someone, but I can't quite put my finger on whom. I shake my head. I have bigger problems.

"Could you please give us some space?" I take one step closer, as if I can intimidate him into vacating his spot.

"Not sure it's smart for you to be next to him before your turn on stage." Wil nods at the number five sticker on my shoulder. His accent is decidedly British. Didn't Jeremiah say this dude was from Germany? Or is Jeremiah too drunk to know the difference between the two countries? "He might just chuck up all over your pretty clothes and ruin your performance before you begin. How about I keep an eye on your boyfriend, and you can talk it out after you're done?"

"No."

"No?" His thick dark eyebrow climbs up, and a smile returns to his face. Maybe it is working on me. Would've worked if I didn't have a drunk Jeremiah and my dreams riding on the line.

"No. He's not my boyfriend. Who has time for that?" Why am I telling him I'm single? Need to focus. "I hired him to play the guitar for me." I raise my splinted fingers and shove them in front of Wil's face. "See?"

"Well, that clears that."

If I expected sympathy from this dude, I didn't get it.

"I don't do the girlfriend thing either. Not planning on starting it now." He licks his lips like I might be his next meal. "Jeremiah might have difficulty standing up, so playing an instrument is bloody unlikely."

"Dammit." I know the guy is right.

We both turn to regard the hoodie-clad Jeremiah, currently staring into his half-empty beer glass as if the golden liquid has the answers to every mystery in life.

"What did you say your name was?" Wil's molten stare focuses on my eyes then my mouth, as if he were ready to catch whatever tumbles out next. And I wish I were here for fun. Hot, kiss-worthy fun.

"El. El Vella." My voice sounds raspier than normal.

His eyes flash back to mine. Something switches in them. He re-surveys me, and his demeanor changes. The relaxed flirty vibe drops as fast as the last note of Dad's latest hit. He loses his smile, the fire in his eyes gone, and for reasons I can't understand, I miss it already.

Wil leans in like he's going to kiss me, his fiery breath tickling my ear instead. Is this his signature move? Is he going to ask me out? Would I say yes? Goosebumps run down my arms, and my heart rises to my throat.

"I know who you are."

END OF SNEAK PEEK

WE Blend
arrives summer 2022.

Add WE Blend to your
Goodreads Reading List
today!

SNEAK PEEK

THE KISS

"KISSES, LIES, & US" SERIES BOOK #1

ONE

NICK

The truth is—I tell lies all the time. What's one more?

I twirl the fake ID my friends gave me for my birthday. It's my face all right, but according to the black block letters on this driver's license, my name isn't Nick, it's Shawn. The address is also not mine, nor the age. I'm newly nineteen, and Shawn's twenty-one. Old enough to drink but not too old for those inclined to question.

I catch the bartender's eye for the third time. A tingle travels down my neck.

She reaches over in front of a woman my mom's age, lays a snowflake-shaped coaster on the bar to my right, and places a fancy pink cocktail with a paper umbrella on it. Glossy green leaves frame the name tag on the pocket of her white resort uniform. The sprig of ivy is the only nod to Christmas Eve. The tag hangs down at an angle, making it hard to read her name, but it begins with an S.

"And what can I get for you?" She hands a glass of sparkling water to a server who appears and disappears to my left. Her voice rings over the smooth jazz. My pulse beats in my ears and dampens the chatter of a couple dozen patrons scattered around the small dimly lit bar.

"Old Fashioned." Dad's been ordering them at every place we've been to this week. This whole trip turned into him showing off that he's landed on his feet. He spends every day trying to get back into Mom's good graces. Bonding time with me doesn't appear to be on the agenda anymore.

"Is that your ID?"

I slide the laminated card her way, and she flicks her eyes between the photo and me. The one-corner-of-the-mouth smile I learned from my brother plus the direct eye contact should project enough confidence to calm any suspicions. I vibrate as if she raised the bass in my chest to high but don't lift my eyebrow or move into full-on flirting. That'd be too much.

"Visiting from Chicago?"

"Yep."

One of those preppy professional-service smiles reveals white teeth that amplify the glow of her sun-kissed face. Lots of hours spent at the tanning booth to get that shade, I bet.

She beams even wider, and I see that one of her canines on top is crooked. You have to pay attention to notice, but now that I do, her whole image changes, and the film of affluence the resort transferred onto her disappears. The tightly wound string inside me slackens.

The bartender hands my fake back. Her fingers are cold and. . . damp? I run my thumb over the ID to remove what I hope is water and slide the card into the pocket of my jacket.

"Sorry." She catches my gesture and wipes her fingers off on a bar towel, reinforcing the humanity behind the uniform. I relax into my seat. "Buffalo Trace or Woodford Reserve?"

What the fuck are those? I flip my phone over. Me, Nick, has no idea what she's asking about, but the twenty-one-year-old Shawn should have an answer.

"Whatever you think's best." Another thing I picked up from Dad. He's been throwing the phrase around, and Mom thinks he's matured. I hope he did. For her sake.

The bartender nods and turns around. While the bulky shirt doesn't reveal much of her body, the black pants hug her butt, and she'd get much better tips displaying that thing to the customers. More of a boob man myself, but I don't discriminate. She stands on her tiptoes to get a bottle with amber liquor from the glass shelf. I should stop staring at how cute her nose looks in profile, or wondering what she would look like in a less bulky top, or looking at her pants. I shift in my seat and try to ignore the flare of heat at the base of my spine. Definitely not looking at those. It's a slippery slope.

I force my eyes away from the perky backside that matches her whole sunny persona and survey the rows of bottles. The bar has no Christmas trees or Santas, going with a snow theme instead. Along the shelves with multi-colored jewel cases containing alcohol lies white fluffy material pretending to be the snow that doesn't exist in LA. A string of large snowflake-shaped lights glows above the top of the bar.

There aren't many things I'll miss about Chicago, but snow on Christmas might be one. I'd have to get used to people walking around in shorts, flip flops, and light sweaters. No matter how festive it is, nothing screams "Christmas" to me in LA.

The blond ponytail above the bartender's shoulders bounces when she moves to get a short tumbler with a line design cut across the bottom. Something James Bond would use. Many steps above the red plastic cups I drink cheap beer out of back home.

She grabs three bottles and sets them next to the glass. It's like I'm watching Mom's favorite British baking show, wondering what's next. I lean in. First, a bit of clear liquid goes in, then water, some dark stuff from a small container with a yellow cap, and a dash from an even tinier one with an orange label. The text on them is too small for me to read to find out what they are. I assumed cocktails could be convoluted, but this looks a bit like my chemistry class. She stirs the mixture with a silver spoon that has a long skinny handle, places one gigantic baseball sized ice cube into the glass, and pours Woodford Reserve over the ice.

Everything she does is self-assured and practiced. She shaves a bit of orange and lemon peel, folds them, runs them around the rim of the glass, squeezes a twist of mist over the whole thing, and places them in next to the ice. The scent of citrus hits my nostrils and sends me back to Yaya slicing lemons from her garden for Psari Plaki. The bartender's tan fingers match my drink but it's her crisp uniform, the glass, and the garnish that make this scene look like everything I'd expected from an overpriced bar at a high-end resort.

"Enjoy." I almost believe she means it. I bite the inside of my cheek as she moves the glass my way.

Ah, here it is. This would be the money shot: her hand setting the drink down as if it's in front of the viewer. The bar top can't be wood. I'd change it to something more reflective, maybe acrylic, so I could play with the lights and reflections.

I narrow my eyes and see the camera moving in as her hand pushes forward with the drink. The contrast of the amber liquid, tan skin, white cuff of the shirt, and touch of yellow and orange from the fruit peels work together to make the shot dramatic. I could underscore this scene with some sick beats as the glass comes toward us, and then something slow as we pan to it.

"Something wrong with the drink?" She leans closer and the foliage moves on the tag, revealing her name. Sarah C.

"Sarah, right? All good, thank you."

Another trick of Dad's. "Call them by their names," he told me yesterday, "the staff appreciates it." The staff. My stomach churns. People like him who come to places like this have staff, listen to smooth jazz, and order drinks you need a degree in mixology to make. He forgets Mom is the staff.

She's been cutting people's hair for the last ten years.

I take a deep breath and rotate the glass. How do I drink this? I've come too far to disappoint Sarah. Am I supposed to sniff it, like Mom does with her wine? I can't remember if Dad did anything special with his. I raise the drink to my lips.

The liquid burns my throat, but I think I hide it well. Lying's always come naturally to me. I get that from Dad too.

I take another gulp. Pretending. One more gulp. Fibbing.

Sometimes I forget who the real Nick is.

And another one. It burns less with every swig, but I hate the taste. Bitterness coats my tongue. I can't drink any more. The glass, however, I love. Maybe I'll buy one like it for myself one day and drink beer out of it.

Why didn't I order a beer and enjoy something I liked instead of pretending I'm sophisticated? For the sake of who? The middle-aged crowd around me? The sunny Sarah, with her big grin and bright blue eyes? Eyes that are checking me out. No. I shake my head. Checking the fancy, Old Fashioned-drinking Shawn out.

Would she like me if I didn't pretend? If, for once, I was just me?

The fake ID can shield the real Nick from potential fallout yet let me be. . . well, me. Minus the right name. I straighten, my brain lighting up at the idea. The little piece of plastic, the small lie offers a chance to not be afraid to be Nick. Be myself.

"Sarah?" I begin my experiment.

From this point on, I vow to only tell the truth.

To this girl.

For this one night.

My heartbeat tries to outrun the tapping of my foot. Bartenders are like shrinks—they're supposed to listen and keep your secrets. Right?

TWO

Sarah

And I thought tonight would be boring.

Pull a double on Christmas Eve, compliment a few drunk lonely men, and make some good tips so I can pay off my overdue cell phone bill. Maybe get back to the apartment and the swinging Christmas Eve party my roommates are holding before someone starts having sex in my bedroom. The plan was simple.

Enter this guy. He's a plot twist in the film noir that was supposed to be my evening. He's all sorts of tall, dark, and handsome dressed in a black jacket and a red T-shirt that's calling to me like a beacon in this sea of winter white.

I swish the martini shaker and watch out of the corner of my eye as Shawn takes a sip of his drink. Did he notice I put a little extra bourbon in? Probably not. Years of bartending to figure out how to pour the perfect shot, but no one notices. They just want to name drop when ordering their fancy drinks. The silver cylinder almost flies out of my grasp, I rattle it so hard. I grit my teeth and restore my customer satisfaction smile. Sometimes I wonder if they even know what it is they're drinking, or if it's just the latest fad.

Shawn rubs the condensation off the smooth tumbler of his Old Fashioned. Up and down. His strong fingers wrap around the crystal. Lucky glass.

Really, Sarah? It's been a bit of a dry spell but c'mon. It's just fingers. And who under forty orders an Old Fashioned?

Old Fashioneds aren't in right now. It's all about gin these days. Thanks, Ryan Reynolds and your millions of Instagram followers. But maybe I should change my lead character's drink from a rum and coke to an Old Fashioned? Make Wesley seem more worldly. Hmmm. Need to think about that.

Sure. I've been *thinking* about Wesley and my opus for two months now. How about writing for a change? That screenplay isn't going to finish itself.

Unlike this martini. I can make 'em in my sleep. Plop, swish, pour.

I turn on my signature smile and focus on delivering a perfect martini to the next customer. In return, I get the glassy-eyed response from the woman sitting next to Shawn. Seeing me, but not seeing me. To her, I'm just another California blonde. That's me, your sweet, valley-girl bartender, here to listen to your woes, offer a kind nod or encouraging word as you spend your evening getting pickled at this swanky resort my poor broke ass couldn't afford to eat at, never mind stay.

Except I'm not sweet or from the valley. No one here notices or cares that I grew up far away in the great white north, as Californians like to joke. No, really, never heard that one before. It was like a daily mantra when I first got here and people remarked on my accent, or rather lack thereof. It's plain Canada to me, where the maple syrup is sweet and people can't look you in the eye when they lie to you. Not like here.

But Shawn's brown eyes didn't look away. The sparkle I see there almost makes me believe he cares enough to know my name.

"Sarah?"

Shawn *did* want to know my name. I sway his way. "Yes, Mr. Old Fashioned."

He swings his head, and I watch his dark hair flop over his forehead. "You're never going to let that go, are you?"

"Well, I call 'em as I see 'em and you . . . you dug your own hole." I bite my lip.

"Seriously, what can I do to change my reputation here? I'm desperate. Give a guy a break." His puppy-dog eyes urge me to give him anything he wants. I grin.

Holy crap. What is wrong with me?

"Fine. Give me something to work with here." I roll my eyes but flash him my real smile. Will he even notice the difference? Wow. Did he just raise an eyebrow at me? I'm seeing things now. "What's your favorite song?"

It's like he struck gold. Or I did. He sits up straight, and I have to look up. The skin on my neck heats. Wow, he is tall. I like tall. Evens out my short. One side of Shawn's mouth curls. Cute. So cute.

"That's a big question. I mean, one song for all time? Too many options." His gaze locks on mine, and his pupils grow as we enter a staring match. "You have to narrow down the playing field a bit. You can't put my latest fave and the Beatles in the same category."

I laugh. I actually laugh. Air rushes into my chest, and I'm giddy. Where did this guy come from?

I place my arms on the bar and lean toward him, waiting to see if he checks out my cleavage. I'm pretty sure he was eyeballing it earlier. They all check out my chest. Maybe I should give him the benefit of the doubt and chalk it up to an attempt to read my nametag. Yeah, right.

Shawn's eyes never leave mine. Okay. The bar behind him falls out of focus. I might need to sit down. "Okay, then. Favorite Christmas song."

Now he laughs. Crinkles form at the corner of his eyes, and the sparkle is back. "Oh, I asked for that, didn't I?'

"Yup." Who am I to disagree?

Tapping his finger—the one previously feeling up his glass—against his bottom lip, Shawn makes a face like he's concentrating hard. Goosebumps rush across my clavicle. I love that he's taking this seriously. He's taking me seriously.

"Well, you know, I like the classics. I'm gonna stay in my lane. *Little Drummer Boy*, wait for it"— his grin is infectious—"*Peace on Earth* by Bowie and Bing." He slaps his hand on the bar, pleased with himself. "Two geniuses of their genres coming together to create magic. That's Christmas to me."

"Who are you?" My mouth takes over.

The light in his eyes dims. No, no, we were having fun. Ignore my stupid question, keep talking about Bowie. I clutch the edge of the bar. My brain scrambles, trying to bring back the sun. "I love Bowie too."

"Just a k . . . guy from Chicago here for the holidays visiting my dad." He rubs the fine layer of stubble on his chin. Would the short hairs be soft, or scratch my fingers? "I'm waiting for him to finish up a meeting."

"The windy city? Enjoying the warm weather?"

"I guess. Doesn't feel like Christmas, though."

"Where I grew up, we always had a white Christmas. We'd go skating on Boxing Day."

Shawn peers at me like I have two heads. "Boxing Day?"

"Keep forgetting you Americans don't celebrate Boxing Day. In Canada, where I'm from"—I point at my chest, but his eyes don't stray— "it's the day after Christmas. You get to lounge around stuffing yourself with leftovers, watching movies, or, if you're like my mom, you throw your kids out into the snow to burn off the sugar we inhaled. I think she wanted some peace and quiet."

Why am I still talking? I pick at a snowflake-shaped coaster. I just shared more with Shawn in two minutes than I did the first six months I lived with my roommates. And I'm pouring the liquor, not drinking it. Yet. One of the perks of this job is sampling new products our boss acquires so we can recommend them. The new Japanese and Belgian beers I'm bringing to the "so you're alone on Christmas too" celebration—the impromptu party my friends Siobhan and Claudia are throwing for out-of-towners—looked promising. Is there even such a thing as a local in LA?

"I can roll with that. Not the sugar, it's not my thing, but the movie part, for sure. I'm either watching one or filming one."

"Well, you're in the right town." I wince at the vinegar in my voice. Really, Sarah, you gotta get over this. It was one bad move. How were you supposed to know it was a scam? Not everyone in Tinseltown is a liar or a crook. Newbies, like Shawn here, start off decent, straightforward, and honest, and he might even stay that way. I shrug. For most of us, this town eventually chews us up and spits us out like yesterday's trash.

"That's my plan. Move here."

Should I burst his bubble? Warn him? Nah, not my place. Shawn has family here. They'll look out for him.

"Hey, Sarah, where d'you want this?" Ryan's holding another box of the wine I asked him to bring from the storeroom. Is it number eight or nine? I'm losing count. I massage my temples. Hope we have enough to last the rest of the night.

"There is fine." I point to the other end of the bar, where the last unopened bottle sits.

"What else do you need help with?" Patience has never been Ryan's virtue. The man can't seem to sit still. "I need to get back to the floor. The VIP group needs attention."

Shit. I survey the dwindling crowd. Standing here just chatting with this Shawn guy isn't good for my tips.

"On my way," I shout to Ryan over my shoulder and give Shawn my best apology smile.

I top off the guy whose attempts at flirting irritated me before Shawn showed up but are ridiculous at this point. He's drinking Veuve like it's water, which is great for the bar, but my skin crawls as he licks his lips while not so subtly staring down the open collar of my uniform. My stomach rolls. I pull the material closed and hoof it down to Ryan to help him unpack the box.

This Icellars Winery's red is popular lately. Another thing from Canada that made it in LA, unlike me. I leave two bottles on the bar as my coworker stacks the rest underneath.

"Got a live one there?" Ryan turns his stoned smirk on me.

"What?"

"The hot kid." My partner for the evening nods in Shawn's direction.

"Him? He's not a kid." Not with that five o'clock shadow.

Ryan narrows his eyes at me like he's got a secret. "Only guy here under fifty. Besides me."

"What's your point, Ryan?" He's a little too aware of my LA loser streak. You could say, he got the ball rolling. We had a thing when I first started—another one of my mistakes. I was so green when I moved out here. All bright-eyed and bushy tailed. Good thing the thick skin grew quickly.

Still, unlike every other aspect of his life, Ryan is pretty mature about being friends. I think. He doesn't seem to mind that I'm basically his boss.

"All I'm saying, I've seen that look before." His eyes dart down the bar to Shawn. "Is he eligible to join the Sarah Club?"

I follow Ryan's gaze. Shawn's honey brown hair flops over his eyes as he studies the half-empty glass he's no longer drinking. Flutters dance at the base of my throat. Good taste in music. Check. Doesn't take himself too seriously. Check. Hands big enough to wrap around my waist. Check.

"Why not?" I scrunch my nose. "Could be fun."

"Attagirl." Ryan grins at me. The same grin that got me in trouble the first time. Good thing it holds no power over me anymore. "Get back on that horse. Ride, baby, ride."

I punch Ryan lightly in the stomach. The flutters spread to my diaphragm as I turn and saunter toward my target. Maybe this Christmas won't suck after all.

THREE

NICK

At the other end of the bar, Sarah's from-under-the-lash, let-me-check-you-out glance is not so subtle. Sarah attempts another sneaky eye-rake. I can't read lips, but I'd bet my left nut the conversation she's having with the surfer dude she's been bossing around is about me. She better be saying something good cause I'm not playing around. What she got was genuine Nick Stavros. No fakeness in sight.

Or was I too eager? Going on about Bing and Bowie. Should have chosen Bieber. He's Canadian. Or anything from the twenty-first century? Something she might like, instead of revealing what Mom calls 'my old soul.' I bounce my knee. Am

I losing my touch? Although the touch has never been me, it's always been whatever the girl was looking for.

Like my last girlfriend, Mackenzie. She wanted a macho-man, a hockey-player with anger issues and aggressive make out sessions, preferably somewhere the right people would see us. Nicky, being the people pleaser extraordinaire, obliged. It did get me access to her dad's video editing studio. No complaints here.

Never had a girl I lost my shit about. Not playing innocent. I have needs and they got met. Mackenzie wanted what I had to offer, and if we helped each other in and out of the bedroom, it only made our relationship more beneficial. No feelings were involved. We both knew what we wanted and got exactly that.

Until I wasn't a hockey player anymore. She ditched me for my former teammate Clark, who was violent and aggressive without any acting needed. That hurt way less than the puck I caught with my face. I trace the scar it left on my cheek. No regrets. I got to use my right hand a bit more in the privacy of my room but appreciated the relief of not wasting my time on a girl I had nothing in common with. Asking her dad to work at his camera shop was not as hard as I thought, so even without Mackenzie, I got access to all the filming equipment I needed.

Damp fingers on my hand. I look up, and Sarah is in front of me. Her eyes search mine. What did I miss? Is she expecting a reaction? A response? I tug on a red cord and the festive music disappears.

"Talking to me?"

"Yes. My shift's ending. Wanna ditch these old folks and hang with some people our age?" She stumbles over her words, they come out so fast.

Well, well. The internal standing ovation I'm imagining boosts me up more than the cheers from the bleachers after a hard check against the boards. The real Nick is not so bad at flirting. Good to know. I remove the second earbud and give her my full attention. Dad expects me to stay close since we're leaving as soon as his meeting is over. But that could be hours. And anything Sarah has to offer is so much more . . . *alluring* for anyone with functioning senses than hanging at this overpriced mausoleum.

"Got something in mind?"

"Yeah." Her mouth turns upward. "My roommates are having a party. The more the merrier."

Party isn't what I had in mind. Something one-on-one would be better, but beggars can't be choosers. The point is, it's still spending time with her.

"Sure," I say.

Her eyes light up at my words. "Great. Give me ten to finish up and change."

"Um, okay." I look around the room. "I'll wait here."

Sarah rounds the bar and sways her hips as she passes by the pool. To work here she has to be at least twenty-one, but I'd swear she's my age, if not younger. She's even tinier than I thought, yet all sides of her look the right contrast of big and small. She'd fit perfectly in my hands. Heat flares across the tips of my fingers, and I tuck them under my thigh before they decide we should follow.

She disappears behind a white door. I put a twenty under my glass.

That could've been a pity invite. I rub the stubble from not shaving since we've arrived in LA. But when she touched my hand—I don't know. The heat travels to my chest and pools there. Something's happening between us.

Either way, it's better than staying here waiting for Dad to finish schmoozing some big-name studio exec, hoping his screenplay sells. I wanted them to drop me off at the beach or the Griffith Observatory, but according to Dad, there's no need to sightsee because I'll get a chance to visit every tourist trap when I move here. I huff. Instead, I was the third wheel on a trip down memory lane for him and Mom.

A hand on my shoulder startles me.

"Shawn?" Sarah's touch is warm and gentle.

My stomach sinks. Shawn. That's me. I forgot I wasn't me—stupid fake ID.

What was I thinking, using it? Oh, right, needed a cool LA story to tell my former teammates. Haven't had the nerve to use the fake back home yet, where someone might recognize me. The guys used my high school yearbook picture. They find it funny to tease me, say I look like Shawn Mendes. There are worse dudes to be compared to. His songs are not my go-to, but his collaboration with Bieber was decent. And who am I to say no to a good fake? At least the last name is clever: Rosstav—an anagram for Stavros, my real surname.

"Sorry it took me so long."

She's changed. And I like it. The damned heat resurges.

The bulky white uniform top is gone, replaced with a much more form-hugging but equally white top drawing the eye to her skin even more. One side of the collar slides down and exposes her tan shoulder and the strap of her bra. The shirt is short enough to reveal a swath of taut midriff, and I ball my hands to keep from touching her.

Her hair is no longer in a ponytail. A smooth gold sheath is gathered over the shoulder that's still covered. And then there's the bottom half of her outfit. The cutoffs are so tight. I've never been this happy to see someone wearing shorts in December. White fabric tennis shoes and a bulky blue sweater draped over her messenger bag complete a look I wouldn't see in Chicago after the first of September.

"Ready to go?"

Am I ever. I push off the barstool and follow. As we leave, I take in the view. She looks even better in denim. I bury my hands in my pockets to cover my reaction. Yep, I'm going to like living in LA.

"Okay if I drive?" she asks.

"Sure."

She taps the remote in her hand, and the headlights on a dark blue car flash. Looks like a Beemer. An old one. Still has that snub-nose look. Yep, there's the blue and white propeller logo on the hood. I skim the cold metal lines of the fender. Can this get any better? She drives a convertible.

I fold myself into the passenger seat, not quite enough space for my long legs, but this ride is worth it. Her car is all sorts of right. Not Mom's embarrassing minivan, a true old-school convertible. I crane my neck to inspect every inch of the interior. Is it too cold to put the top down?

Kelly Clarkson blasts a high note of *Silent Night* as Sarah starts the car. Her hand shoots out and turns down the volume. "Sorry, I like to feel my music."

I like this girl. "Totally get it." I lift my red earbuds. "Same. Mom says I'll regret it when I'm her age and need a hearing aid, but that's for the old N . . . me to worry about." Fuck. I almost slipped. This was too close.

"D'you live with your mom?"

The first instinct is to embellish, to fall into the comfort of my old Nicky habit, and lie about a place of my own. That'd be easy. But tonight is about the truth. Let's test the waters.

"For now."

"That's smart." She doesn't seem bothered. "The best way to save money if you can do it. I did too, until my move to LA."

I uncurl my fingers and rub my sweaty palms on my jeans. That wasn't bad. Actually, it was good. Felt good to tell the truth.

Sarah shifts the car into first, and it jerks.

"Manual? Wow."

"My dad insisted I learn, and then I liked it. Old Betty here and I have been together for a long time." She pats the steering wheel before shifting gears again.

"You named your car?"

"You haven't?"

"I . . . I don't have a car." I relax into the seat. Not trying to talk my way around lies is freeing. Way to keep this honesty ball rolling.

"Oh. Sorry. I always assume everyone has a car. It's essential in LA."

"I'll put it on my 'move to LA' list. You drove this here from . . ."

"Toronto. Yup. See?" She points to the dashboard. "The speedometer's in kilometers."

Not gonna resist that invite. My pulse quickens. I bend over to look at the speedometer—and her—closer, but it's my nose that gets a treat. She smells like strawberries as I breathe her in. Blood rushes many places at once. Sarah's scent is the only part of her I can access freely. The rest of her is not mine to enjoy. It doesn't make me want her any less.

I lean in more, but that only makes things worse. The closeness is torture. Sweet, sweet torture. This pain I can take. Or end, if she'd be interested. If I closed the distance between us, my mouth would land on her neck, and I could draw a map with my kisses from the soft hollow under her ear over her jaw and to her lips.

My stomach rumbles.

Did she hear it? I hope not. Even though the only edible thing I've had since lunch five hours ago were the free pretzels at the bar, and I tend to care about food as much as a hungry hippo, right now I don't want anything to distract me from the exposed skin that I'm becoming obsessed with.

Maybe the drink on an empty stomach is to blame for how attracted I am to Sarah and how carefree and comfortable it is to be around her. I tear myself away and rest my back against the cool leather of the seat, as if it can chill my fevered fantasies.

Another rumble, but it's not my stomach this time.

"Was that you again or me?" She pokes my leg. I catch the white of her teeth on her lower lip. "I'm starving. Mind if we stop for something to eat first?"

Is she kidding? If I can't have her, I might as well be fed. The salad with chicken strips Mom insisted I order at lunch left me hungry before we left the swanky restaurant. Starving doesn't even cover it. Play it cool.

"I could eat." It's the truth.

"I know a food truck with the best tacos. It's near Griffith Park. Have you seen the view from the observatory yet?"

Baby, I've seen it all is what the sophisticated Shawn would probably say.

"Haven't seen much of anything." My uncensored words are flowing now.

Her mouth turns down a little at the edges. I've screwed up. I clutch the grab handle. I knew this was too good to be true.

"That sucks. LA has so much to offer." She's not mad. "When I first got here, I wandered around awestruck for weeks. I can give you a tour, if you like. How long are you in town for?"

I hate my dad. Why do we have to leave tonight?

"I'd love that. But my dad rented a house in Santa Barbara." It's the same place the four of us spent our last Christmas in together as a family. Mike and I had fun learning to surf. Of course, that was before. Before the truth came out and banished my big bro, Mom, and me to Chicago. The weight I've been carrying on my shoulders for ten years presses down. "We're going there tonight and flying back home the day after Christmas."

"Oh." Does she sound disappointed, or am I imagining it? She drums her fingers on the steering wheel. "Too bad. Maybe next time."

"Totally. I'm hoping to move here next summer."

She rewards me with another smile.

END OF SNEAK PEEK

Kisses, Lies, & Us

arrives fall 2022.

Add Kisses, Lies, & Us: The Kiss to your Goodreads Reading List today!

CPSIA information can be obtained
at www.ICGtesting.com
Printed in the USA
JSHW020058050523
41291JS00003B/190

9 781957 897004